"You need to stop running and make a stand. But you need men."

John flashed a grin at Zee. "You need me."

"No. You need to get out of here."

He stared down at her, rooted firmly in place. "I'm not going anywhere without you."

"But you are. Please, leave."

"Some of those men were headed in the direction of my place last night. They probably already know who I am."

"They have no reason to come after you unless you're with me, but it's best that you don't go home for a few days."

"In the movie, did the Warriors win in the end?"

"Yeah. They did."

"How? Did they do it alone while scattered, or together working as a team?"

"I can't turn to the rest of my team." They were all in hiding, supposedly off the grid, and she didn't know where.

"All the more reason you need me. You can't do this alone."

ALASKAN CHRISTMAS ESCAPE

JUNO RUSHDAN

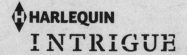

This is for my little ones, K. and A. Thank you for your patience
and for being my biggest cheerleaders.

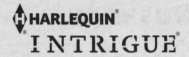

ISBN-13: 978-1-335-48929-6

Alaskan Christmas Escape

Copyright © 2021 by Juno Rushdan

Recycling programs
for this product may
not exist in your area.

For questions and comments about the quality of this book,
please contact us at CustomerService@Harlequin.com.

Harlequin Enterprises ULC
22 Adelaide St. West, 40th Floor
Toronto, Ontario M5H 4E3, Canada
www.Harlequin.com

Printed in U.S.A.

Juno Rushdan is the award-winning author of steamy, action-packed romantic thrillers that keep you on the edge of your seat. She writes about kick-ass heroes and strong heroines fighting for their lives as well as their happily-ever-afters. As a veteran air force intelligence officer, she uses her background supporting Special Forces to craft realistic stories that make you sweat and swoon. Juno currently lives in the DC area with her patient husband, two rambunctious kids and a spoiled rescue dog. To receive a FREE book from Juno, sign up for her newsletter at junorushdan.com/mailing-list. Also be sure to follow Juno on BookBub for the latest on sales at bit.ly/BookBubJuno.

Books by Juno Rushdan

Harlequin Intrigue

Fugitive Heroes: Topaz Unit

Rogue Christmas Operation
Alaskan Christmas Escape

A Hard Core Justice Thriller

Hostile Pursuit
Witness Security Breach
High-Priority Asset
Innocent Hostage
Unsuspecting Target

Tracing a Kidnapper

Visit the Author Profile page at Harlequin.com.

CAST OF CHARACTERS

Zenobia "Zee" Hanley—The hotshot hacker is a former CIA operative on the run. She has lots of secrets and is willing to die to protect those she loves. But when she sees a chance to prove her team's innocence, she'll risk everything to pursue it.

John Lowry—He's a retired SEAL, struggling to find a new sense of normal since his medical discharge. His quiet life out in the remote wilderness takes a life-altering turn as he chooses to help a beautiful neighbor in need.

Ryker Rudin—Team leader of the CIA strike force sent to eliminate Zee. This mission is also deeply personal for him and he'll stop at nothing to get the job done.

Mike Cutler—Best friend of John. He'll do whatever he can to help a buddy.

David Bertrand—A CIA analyst who was fired under suspicious circumstances.

Hunter Wright—Former leader of Team Topaz. Every member of his unit he loves like family. The most important thing to him is keeping them safe.

Gage Graham—Good friend and former colleague of Zee.

Chapter One

You're a fugitive, Zenobia Hanley reminded herself. Getting in any deeper with this man, regardless of how amazing he was, would only end in disaster. Might even get him killed.

"Thanks for the wonderful meal," she said, washing the last plate and handing it to John.

"All I did was cook the roast." Drying the dish, he smiled, a charming flash of white teeth that never failed to make her heart flutter. "You made everything else, and it was excellent as usual." His grin grew wider and that flutter inside her spread deeper.

Taking the wineglass from her hand, he brushed his fingers across hers. Their gazes caught and held. His grass-green eyes sparkled in the warm firelight of the room.

Zee struggled to keep her thoughts silent, but they leaked out like the water running through her fingers. "We should do this again tomorrow."

His smile faltered. He turned, putting the dishes away. "Two days in a row?" He gave a low whistle. "When we started this arrangement, you made it clear that once a week, for a game of chess, was more than enough. I've respected that."

Chess had turned into lunch. Lunches into dinners.

"I was being careful," she admitted. "A city girl, alone, in the remote wilderness. I didn't want to give you the wrong impression." To show any hint of weakness, no vulnerability, especially to a man who had a coiled readiness to him, reflexes honed to a razor-sharp edge. "That was before we became friends and I got to know you." Now she was confident he was one of the good guys. Even though he had secrets and a past, too. None of which he wanted to discuss any more than she did. "It's the holidays. Besides, we see each other three or four days a week as is."

"While trading, my goods for yours. A shared cup of coffee in between. Fishing when the weather is good. Not this."

Something inside her sank. Their time together was starting to change. Evolve. Their get-togethers felt less casual and more romantic each time. That wasn't healthy for either of them.

"You're right." She dried her hands on a towel. "Sorry for suggesting we break a rule I set." But she liked *this*. She liked *him*. *A lot*. Despite her best intentions, she'd grown to rely on John, for far more than game meet and chopped firewood. "Let's forget it."

Grabbing her coat from the back of a chair, she turned to leave, which was for the best.

"Don't misunderstand me." John put a hand on her shoulder, turning her around. He stared at her, really studying her, as if what he was about to say next mattered. "It is the holidays." He dropped his hand. "I'd love to do this tomorrow. I'll make venison stew. How about we do it at your place?"

She had changed the boundaries, and now he was testing to see how far they could be stretched. She slipped on her parka. "Is it okay if we hang out here again?"

Being able to make a graceful exit whenever she needed was important. No hurt feelings. No pressure.

His brow furrowed as he raked a hand through his shaggy light brown hair. "Why don't we ever spend time inside your house?"

She shrugged. "Your place is cozier." She glanced around at his framed photos of family and friends hung on the walls and at the hand-stitched quilt that his mother had made for him draped on the back of the sofa.

John was shrewd and if he spent enough time in her place, he'd eventually notice that she lived like a ghost. Not a hint of anything personal in the space. Her cabin was a sterile showroom that would make him uneasy after a few hours. Cause him to ask questions.

There were countless reasons why they didn't need to hang out in her cabin.

"Okay." He flashed an easy grin. "But come the New Year, we should shake things up."

She'd worry about that next year. "Let's make a whole day out of it. Begin with scones or maple pecan sticky buns."

"I love those fancy biscuits, but I want the sticky buns."

"Fresh rosemary bread to go with the stew. For dessert, I can make apple pie."

"My mouth is watering already, but you're spoiling me."

"I'm doing no such thing. You hunt and chop the wood. I go into town for essentials you can't forage, and I ply you with all the home-baked goods you can handle. That's our deal."

Fishing was as far as she was willing to go to become a wilderness woman while John wasn't much for baking and avoided going into Fairbanks at all costs.

"At the irresistible rate you're going, I don't know if I'll be able to keep my willpower in check and my waistline from expanding." John put a hand to his taut belly that was in no danger of getting flabby anytime soon.

"You have nothing to worry about." Zee patted his chest without thinking, and he covered her hand with his, holding her palm there. The isolation, the great expanse of wilderness got to her sometimes, had her craving the barest physical contact. So, she allowed herself to enjoy the hard contours beneath his turtleneck as he tensed and leaned into her touch. He had a heavily muscled frame. Up close he was imposing, in a sexy way. "You look great."

Warmth from the hearth curled around them. The soft amber glow played over his features. The term *ruggedly handsome* didn't do this man justice.

But she had made a horrible mistake once in getting involved with the wrong guy. A gross error in judgment that haunted her to this day, making her doubt whether a *normal* relationship was possible.

John was different, on a cellular level, from the monster who had hurt her, but it didn't change the fact that she was on the run. Her situation alone made any relationship impossible.

Stop courting disaster. "It's late." Already after eleven.

She lowered her hand and put on her gloves. John followed her to the door.

Smiling down at her, he took the wool cap hanging from her pocket and tugged it over her curls that she'd corralled into a ponytail. As he lowered his hands, he grazed her ears and cheeks. The contact was light and brief, and more than enough to make her breath catch and belly tighten.

"I can walk you home," he said, his voice gravelly and low.

"No need." Her place was less than a quarter mile cutting through the woods on foot. Not to mention she had the loaded Beretta she carried everywhere in her coat pocket. In Alaska, it was odd if you weren't always armed. One of the reasons she'd chosen to hide out up here. "It's snowing again. I remember the weather makes your leg ache."

He dropped his gaze and stepped back. "My leg only aches when rain and trouble are coming." His tone turned flat and dry. "For some reason, the snow doesn't bother me too much." He cracked the door open, letting in a bitter December breeze. "I'll see you tomorrow. I'm looking forward to it. To the sticky buns. You're an amazing cook."

Zee's heart shriveled like a dried prune and she knew it wouldn't plump back up until she saw John's smile again. "You're too kind," she said, equally flat, regretting that she'd chosen a humdrum word for the most captivating man she'd ever met.

He pulled up her faux-fur-lined hood over her head. "If you need me for anything, just give me a holler on the radio."

"Sure." She kept her two-way radio on her nightstand within easy reach. "Good night." She felt like a hug—a platonic one; some simple gesture was in order, but she stuffed her hands in her pockets, curling her fingers around the hilt of her gun instead.

"'Night, Zee," he said with a tip of his head.

She hurried out, and when she glanced back, the door was closed.

Bracing against the brutal slap of the cold, she ran down the porch steps and trotted through the snow, taking the same path she followed several times a week.

Had the comment about his leg triggered the abrupt goodbye? She simply hadn't wanted him to go to the trouble of walking her home in this snow.

When had showing consideration become a faux pas?

She'd gleaned he was ex-military from the way he carried himself and fluidly used military jargon and guessed that it wasn't his choice to leave the service. He never talked about it. Or how he had injured his leg. He had an easy, self-assured gait and no hint of a limp unless he'd been sitting for a long time. Even then it disappeared after a minute or two and he was a good runner. Though she suspected the act brought him some discomfort. One night after too much wine, he'd made a comment about his disability check and she'd put the pieces together.

But like John, she had too much respect to pry. There was also the fact that asking questions invited the tables to turn. Her answers would only expose him to unnecessary trouble.

On her porch, she stomped most of the snow off her boots. She hurried inside, then shut the door behind her. The knifelike chill that had settled in her bones started to drain as she soaked in the festive glow of the Christmas lights that she'd strung up in the living room.

She longed to be with her family. How she missed them. All of them.

Peeling off her coat, she removed her gun from the pocket. She tossed the parka onto a chair and slipped the weapon into the back of her waistband.

In the kitchen, she got a drink of water to combat having too much wine with dinner.

Her gaze fell to her laptop on the table and she cursed her talent. Her gift.

Hacking wasn't something she did, it was who she was, and it posed the biggest danger to her, but it might be the only way to clear her name. She'd give anything to have her life restored.

Her entire team had been forced to flee. Zee might be able prove their innocence if given the chance. Already she'd risked everything by digging where she shouldn't. She'd found important breadcrumbs. Now she had to follow the trail and see where it led.

She trudged into her bedroom and plopped down on her bed. Glancing at the handheld radio on her nightstand, she contemplated calling John. Have him come over and make her forget about her troubles. In a different universe, she would, but in this one, she was a fugitive who needed to be ready to run at a moment's notice.

If she slept with John, gave him her heart and then had to bolt later, she'd be tempted to say goodbye and offer some brief explanation. Not simply disappear without a word. The time it'd take, two minutes, ten, to say farewell could mean the difference between life and death.

RYKER RUDIN WASN'T a patient man, but it was more efficient to wait for his team to round up all the civilians on the premises before he got down to the business of killing.

Give his spiel once and then the first bullet would have the biggest impact. This boiled down to professional expediency.

The back outer door of the hackerspace opened, letting in an Arctic gust of late-night air that tasted of pine. His man, Delta Three—code names only on a mission—hauled in the last person here tonight. Officially the 24/7 lab was a community space for like-minded people with common interests such as computers, technology and digital art.

Unofficially, it was a space for hackers. The name was a bit on the nose in his opinion.

Delta Three shoved the sobbing woman who had made a run for it down to the floor. With her palms raised, she crouched beside the others, all trembling together in a huddle.

Ryker, known as Delta Prime for this CIA assignment, crossed his legs and swung the muzzle of the gun toward the group.

The five technophiles shrank back, cowering as if a bullet might fly at any second.

It could.

Eyeing them one by one, Ryker withdrew the sound suppressor from the pocket of his leather trench coat and attached it to the threaded barrel. "Whether or not I kill you is your choice. Tell me what I need to know and I won't shoot you. I'm looking for a woman. Zenobia Hanley," he said, and a knee-jerk spike of lust tangled inextricably with the ever-constant rage flowing through his veins.

A flurry of memories flashed like lightning. Holding her in bed, their sweat-covered bodies pressed close. The look in her eyes, once filled with affection for him. Her unthinkable betrayal that had left him gutted. Furious.

Ryker swallowed the bitter taste in his mouth. "Light brown complexion, brown eyes, long, dark curly hair. Slim build. Hers is not a face you'd soon forget." Maybe never regardless how hard you tried. He gestured to Delta Seven to show her picture. "I need to know how often she's been here and where I can find her. She may be going by a different name. Might prefer to be called Zee."

The twentysomething blond guy lowered his head

and squeezed his eyes shut, jaw clenching before he was shown the picture. He was the one they needed. Blondie knew her.

Ryker stood and stalked closer. Aimed his weapon at the woman who had been brought in last. "Someone better start talking, or I start shooting."

One. Two. Three. He pulled the trigger. A single bullet spat from the end of the long black barrel, and the woman collapsed. The others screamed and sniveled, clutching one another as if there were safety in numbers. There wasn't.

Ryker stepped in front of the next person. Lowered the muzzle to his forehead.

"Wait!" Blondie said. "Please, stop. She goes by Zee. No last name. She was in here earlier and yesterday, too. Over the past nine months or so, she comes in every two or three weeks. Except for this month. She started coming in several times a week."

"Why the change?" Ryker asked.

"I think she was close to finding something big. But she was scared to dig. Afraid to stay online too long for any given period."

Fear was a survival instinct, and when heeded, it kept you alive. Her fear had been justified. She had dug too deep for too long.

The CIA had caught her yesterday and unleashed Ryker's team for cleanup—a palatable euphemism for assassination. He wouldn't rest until he reclaimed what she'd stolen from him.

Then he would kill her. Slowly. Brutally. Preferably with his bare hands. His vengeance had been a long time coming. "Does she ever come in with anyone or only on her own?"

"Always alone."

"Where can I find her?"

"I don't know." Blondie shrugged. "I swear."

Ryker pulled the trigger, executing a redhead.

"Please!" Blondie raised his palms. "Don't do this. She'll be back in a few days. Just stick around and wait."

What a brilliant idea. His team could cram into the local hotel and roast marshmallows while twiddling their thumbs.

"We're on a tight schedule." Ryker clasped his wrist in front of him and tapped the sound suppressor against his leg. "She may not have told you the name of the town she lives in, but I assure you she's given you enough information to help us zero in on her residence." Zee was a natural chatter, made friends wherever she went. Being on the run, separated from the rest of her old team, she would be inclined to strike up conversations with regular faces. "She lives in a town with no internet, correct?"

Blondie nodded. "Yes, yes. That's why she comes here."

She didn't want the constant temptation of being able to get online. Smart. "How long is the drive for her?"

"Uh, an hour in the summer. With snow it takes her longer. Last time, she mentioned maybe an hour and a half."

"Does she own or rent?"

"She rents, I think. A small cabin."

"Did she ever mention a particular route she takes, the 2 or 3?"

"I don't know," Blondie cried. "Please."

They always became whiny, falling back on useless entreaties. Ryker lowered to a knee and cupped the man's face in his leather-gloved hand. "Shh. Calm down. Think. Route 2 or 3."

Blondie sucked in a shaky breath. "She complained about the late plow of a road once. The 2, I believe. Yeah, that was it."

"That puts her north of Fairbanks," Ryker said to his team, and Delta Ten continued inputting all the information in their shared database with the agency. Their designated intelligence analyst was working this in real time. They would collate the data, scan rental records, date of occupancy, owners who accepted cash on a month-to-month basis, and cross-reference it with roads and terrain to pinpoint the needle in the haystack. The more data the better. "What does she drive?"

"A silver pickup. Old. Ford."

Good. A vehicle parked outside a residence was useful when verifying the location on satellite imagery.

"Did she ever mention a view where she lives?"

"It's Alaska—everyone has a view."

Ryker sighed. "A particular mountain. A lake. River. Campground. Forest."

"Yeah. A neighbor taught her to fish. She's in walking distance to a large pond or a lake and a river. The Chatanika."

Fishing? Zee wasn't an outdoorsy woman but perhaps being forced to live in the boondocks to stay off the CIA's radar inspired changes. "Name of the neighbor?"

"John something or other. A disabled vet. Helpful guy."

One look at Zee would turn an uncooperative curmudgeon into an accommodating fool. Ryker bet the man had been helpful indeed.

Delta Ten nodded. "We've got her location."

Faster than Ryker had expected. Then again, the area was sparsely populated, even more so outside the city, and rentals on the outskirts were bound to be limited.

"Are you going to kill me?" Blondie asked.

"No, I won't." Ryker patted his cheek. "I'm a man of my word." He was, and hope had been necessary to elicit honest answers. But none of the technophiles would survive. Once his team was finished, the place would be torched. "Delta Fifteen will kill you." Four pips in rapid succession followed, and the hackers slumped over, dead. "We'll hit her location at 0200," Ryker said to his entire team over comms, preferring to wait until the wee hours. "Catch the target while she's sleeping. You're free to wound her. I don't care how badly, so long as it's not fatal. I want to look that traitor in the eyes right before I kill her. So she knows that it was me."

"I'M LOOKING FORWARD to the sticky buns," John Lowry muttered under his breath.

You should've kissed her, you idiot.

Sticky buns?

John had sat in front of the fire for hours, replaying the evening, and he was still berating himself.

Zee was wicked smart, cool in a cosmopolitan way that screamed she didn't belong out in the Last Frontier, and one hell of a chess player. A real knockout, too, way out of his league.

Runner's physique. Smooth skin the color of wet sand. A Cupid's-bow mouth. Almond-shaped eyes. Her hair was stunning, especially when she left it loose and wild. He'd never seen anything like it. A magnificent mass of dark spiral curls that he ached to wrap his fingers around and feel spread across his bare chest, sliding over his belly.

Maybe he should traipse down to her house and knock on the door. She might open it wearing her nightgown and a smile, those curls loose around her shoulders. Take his hand and lead him to her bedroom.

He glanced at the clock. Two in the morning. She'd be more likely to open the door with a loaded gun and a scowl and rightfully so.

Growling in frustration, he picked up the silly romance novel Zee had given him as a lark, which he'd been stupid enough to read, and tossed it into the fire.

Zee was wary, her guard always up. Everything she had told him tonight about being more comfortable around him had made sense.

The Alaskan wilderness held extra dangers for women. Not long after moving here he'd learned that this state had the highest rate of rape in the country. Getting to know him and discover he was a decent guy had probably been a delicate balancing act for her. One he respected. Still, he sensed there was a deeper reason behind the boundaries she'd created. She was running, hiding, the same as him.

His demons were personal. There was something inside him that he couldn't switch off, something restless, bred by the military and capable of ugly things for the right reasons. But Uncle Sam no longer wanted him. Had stripped him of his purpose and put him out to pasture.

Forty years old, retired and miserable.

Loneliness was bad, but Zee kept him from reflecting on the misery. The only time he felt alive, happy, these days was when he was with her. In her absence, he was aware of the gaping hole in his life.

He believed her demons were of a physical nature. The giveaway was the perimeter intruder alarms she had set up in the woods around the vicinity of her place. Shortly after she'd moved in, he'd spotted them mounted to the trees. He suspected she might be out here taking such precautions because of an acrimonious breakup. Maybe she had an ex stalking her.

John looked at the mini decorated Christmas tree she had given him to spruce up his place for the holidays. He smiled, though his chest ached.

He didn't want to ruin what was real with her for what might be possible. Yes, he wanted to hold her, make love to her until they were both sated, share the things on his mind that he kept bottled up. Which was bananas since they hadn't even hugged much less kissed.

And what woman in her prime wanted a broken man like him anyway? A washed-up vet, almost ten years her senior, booted from the service for a bum leg and PTSD.

He wanted Zee in his life in any capacity, even if it was only platonic.

A cold shower was what he needed. Though it was a temporary fix. Come tomorrow, one look at her, one hair-flip over her shoulder, one whiff of her skin—coconut and flowers, she smelled like a vacation destination he never wanted to leave—one lick of her tongue across her lips, and he would be a hot mess of a man yearning for something he couldn't have.

John stood, stretching out his stiff right leg. A brutal throb ran from his thigh through his knee to the tibia—the particular ache that forecasted rain.

Or trouble.

A shower and sleep would do him good. Tackle the next day with a clear head. He'd take a long walk before she came over so he could keep up his streak of not needing his medication.

Stretching, he crossed the room and then stopped.

Instinct kicked in before his ears caught the sound. The telltale *whomp-whomp-whomp* was quiet. Too quiet to be military. Or search and rescue. After eighteen years in Special Forces and three living out in the Alaskan wilderness, he knew the difference. If music had been playing or he had been asleep, he would have missed the sound entirely.

That *whomp-whomp* was getting louder, resonating in his soul.

He snatched his down jacket from the hook, stepped out onto his porch and searched the night sky. Clouds obscured the aurora borealis that would otherwise be visible. He took a deep breath, scanning carefully, and waited. The hair on the back of his neck stood on end and it had nothing to do with the crisp, frigid air vibrating around him.

Where is it? Where is it? Where—

Ah, there it is. At his three o'clock.

A black helicopter cut through the sky.

His heart thudded as the chopper took a position over the woods, where it hovered in the scant moonlight. From the outline of the unmarked helicopter, it didn't look like law enforcement. Possibly foreign. He couldn't be sure, but it was unusual.

Four ropes dropped, dangling from the aircraft.

His brain recoiled, yet what he was seeing registered. This was a covert operation. But there was something very wrong about it that gnawed at him.

In his gut, all the way down to the ache in his leg, he sensed this was bad.

Men in tactical gear rappelled down each rope. Close to Zee's place. So close they wouldn't trigger the perimeter alarms she had put up farther out.

Ice water rushed in John's veins. *Zee.*

The four men touched the ground. Red laser sights popped on. Then four more rappelled from the helicopter.

Ah, hell.

Lights came down the main road. Two vehicles stopped and killed their headlights. Once again near Zee's. The ice water in his veins froze solid. How many of them were there?

They weren't SWAT, not police nor FBI. Of that

he was certain. He didn't know who they were, but he did know that they were a strike team of some kind, heading for Zee.

His heart was hammering now. A warning chill rippled down his spine, telling him not to stand by and let whatever was happening simply unfold. It was instinctual, and he'd always trusted his instincts.

He had to get to her, which meant going through them, but there was no way he'd make it to Zee in time before those men reached her place.

Chapter Two

"Zee."

She roused at the sound of John's voice calling her name. Rolling over, she reached for him, but only found a cold, empty side of the bed.

Groaning, she opened her eyes. *No John.* She was alone and dreaming about him again.

"Zee!" His voice was low and harsh with urgency.

She jackknifed up in her bed and grabbed the walkie-talkie. "What's wrong, John? Are you okay?"

"They're coming for you. Closing in fast. Hot and heavy. Get out of the house. Now. Go west."

A fist of ice clenched in her gut. Why hadn't her alarms gone off?

She dropped the radio. Tugged on her jeans and boots. Whipped off her nightgown, trading it for the cashmere sweater that she'd taken off last night. She snatched the gun from the nightstand.

Her gaze cut over her coat on a chair in the living room, to the kitchen. Her laptop was in there. Traces of *everything* she'd looked up were still on the hard drive.

Movement outside her window seized her attention. Her eyes strained to see into the murky shadows.

She spotted the dark silhouettes of two men, coming up onto her porch. Red laser sights from their automatic weapons sliced through the air.

Damn it. There was no time.

She ducked low and bolted for her closet. Inside on the floor was a door she had installed. Not an easy task and one that had taken her days to get it right. She lifted the door without making a sound thanks to the WD-40 she used on the hinges every other week planning for this very eventuality.

Preparation drove her to stay in peak physical condition. Hours of training every single day. Running with a thirty-pound pack on her back, double what she might have to haul for real. Push-ups, sit-ups, pull-ups, burpees. Krav Maga classes in Fairbanks to stay sharp. She had to be ready in case this happened.

The front door squeaked open and the floorboards she'd deliberately loosened creaked under the heavy footfalls, revealing the enemy's location with every step.

Closing the door behind her, she ducked down into the crawl space.

She counted as she crept on her hands and knees through the dark, hollow area between the ground and the floor of the cabin. Once she reached ten, she stretched out her right hand and her fingers closed around her emergency go bag—a duffel made of laminated, high-density nylon that was impenetrable to nature's assaults and contained everything she needed to run.

The boards above her groaned as dust fell, clogging the air. She held her breath rather than dare risk a cough or sneeze that would give away her position.

From the sounds overhead, four men were in the house now, searching the rooms.

Zee unzipped her go bag and ran through the protocol she had rehearsed numerous times blindfolded, anticipating a real scenario would require her to do it at night in the pitch-black dark. She threw on the bulletproof vest that had zippered sides instead of noisy Velcro. On one hip, she attached the holster with her telescopic baton. On the other, she hooked the specially designed holster that held a suppressed 9mm.

She dumped the Beretta inside the bag and made a quick sightless check by hand of the rest of her gear.

Grabbing the *create-a-distraction* device, she tugged on a streamlined coat, thankful she'd packed one to blend in with the snow. She pocketed the device, dropped to her belly and slipped her arms through the straps of the duffel that weighed exactly fifteen pounds, wearing the bag like a backpack.

"Prime, this is Delta Two. The target isn't here," a man said from inside the house. "But the bed is still warm, and we found a laptop."

Damn. How sloppy of her not to scrub the computer clean earlier before dashing off to John's. She had been so excited to see him for dinner, but at the very least, she should've brought the laptop into the bedroom like she did most nights.

Rule number one on the run—no margin for error. She had broken it, messing up big time. Such a stupid mistake that could cost her what she cared about most in the world.

Zee waited to hear a response from Prime, but didn't, so the reply must have been given over their comms.

That meant whoever was leading this Delta kill team was out in the woods somewhere.

"Understood," Delta Two said.

Furniture was tipped over clunking to the floor. They were looking for her escape door to follow her tracks.

Zee low crawled to the west exit of her hidey-hole and pulled the wood cutout in toward her since the snow on the other side was pressed against the foundation. She burrowed out with her bare hands, wishing she had packed spare gloves, and peeked both ways.

Men wearing night-vision goggles were searching the woods. Multiple red beams swept all around. The combination of their NVGs and laser sights gave them every advantage, not including the sheer number of them.

She steadied her breath, bracing herself, and waited for the right moment to move. The device in one hand and her suppressed weapon in the other. Her field of view was limited with threats lurking beyond her vantage point.

Now this was instinct. Prey trying to escape predator.

Another long, deep breath, silencing the whisper of fear, oxygenating her blood and stoking her adrenaline to a pure white heat. When her opening came, she scurried from under the house, scrambled up the mound of snow and bolted for the forest.

Bullets bit into the trees behind her. She kept running, her head low, zigzagging to avoid getting shot, but she never slowed.

Grasping hold of the device in her pocket, she pressed the remote trigger. Explosives she had rigged under the cabin detonated.

The explosion shook the earth, ripping the front door off its hinges and knocking anyone close by off their feet as the house went up in a fireball. Fragments of wood and stone blew a good fifty feet into the air, pelting the surrounding ground.

The blast would have killed anyone inside, and the pandemonium would buy her a few precious seconds. If she was lucky, they hadn't had a chance to get the laptop out. She prayed that was the case.

She pressed on, headed west, like John had told her to go, toward his house. Slim chance the CIA kill team had been tuned in to the two-way frequency since they were dialed into their own comms.

Still, danger would follow her for certain. She didn't want to put John at risk. But his cabin sat on a hill at an advantage. Also, he had spotted the team inbound and had warned her. He had some idea of what was out in these woods stalking her.

Don't think.

Keep moving.

Breathe.

Run.

A twig snapped on her left.

She spun in a crouch toward the sound, gun at the ready. Squeezed the trigger.

The first bullet struck her pursuer in the shoulder, throwing off his aim. On a bended knee, she stabilized her gun hand with a two-hand hold, exhaled and fired.

A clean head shot.

Before she could fully stand and pivot, someone struck her in a football tackle from the side, taking her down to the cold ground.

He was big and heavy. Another one from the tactical team.

She raised her gun, angling for a shot around his body armor and going for his neck. But he seized her wrist and pinned her with his body weight, squeezing the air from her chest. She dug her heels in the snow and bucked her hips up, struggling to move him. To shift the slab of muscle a few inches, giving her the latitude to throw a knee to his groin.

He bore down harder, not allowing her the slightest chance to maneuver.

In this wrestling match, he outweighed and outmuscled her.

There was no contest. Were their orders to kill her on sight, or torture her first for information about the whereabouts of the remaining members of Team Topaz?

No matter what, she'd never talk. She'd fight to the death to protect those she loved. Delta could go to hell, and she'd take out as many of them as she could right along with her.

He slammed her wrist against the forest floor, trying to get her to drop her weapon. She tightened her grasp. Two rounds went off, hit a tree.

If he disarmed her, it was game over and she was as good as dead.

She relaxed her arms, but not the hand clenched around her gun, and stopped struggling, pretending to relent. He rotated as if preparing to stand and she launched her knee up between his legs with all her might.

His breath hissed out, his eyes rolled up into the back of his head, his whole body tensed from the excruciating pain only a man could understand. She slammed the heel of her palm up into his nose, thrusting him to the side. Scrambling to her feet, she came face-to-face with another one from Delta. He already had her locked in his sights, finger on the trigger.

Zee's stomach bottomed out. Every muscle clenched, a blade of fear slicing through the adrenaline, chilling her heart.

There was nothing she could do.

Someone swept up behind the man with the lightning speed of a shadow.

John. He threw a kick to the back of the guy's knee, bringing him down, and flipped off the tactical helmet and then struck him across the skull with a gun, knocking the guy out cold.

She exhaled with momentary relief and ran to John. They locked eyes for a suspended instant as he took her hand, his fingers closing around hers. Something gave way under the strain and washed over her. A startling sense that everything would be okay if they were together.

"What's going on?" John whispered. "Who are these men? Are you in trouble with the law?"

"They aren't law enforcement and I'm no criminal. I promise you." Her gaze fell and she saw it.

A red laser dot on his chest.

Zee lunged in front of John, putting herself between him and the bullet.

The first slug that struck her chest hit her harder than a punch, stealing her breath. The tremendous impact of the second twisted her sideways and dropped her like a sack of potatoes.

It hurt like hell. Shockwaves of pain coursed through her stunned body, her vision blurred, her mind reeling. She wanted to move, to fight, but she could barely breathe.

A tear leaked from her eye as sounds of a struggle filled her ears. She had to get up. To help John. The gun was still in her hand, but she couldn't wiggle a finger.

Quick, brutal blows resounded, fists pummeling flesh. Then there was the crunch of bone snapping.

Her heart quivered.

Not John. Please! Not because of me.

A body hit the ground beside her with a thud. Black tactical gear. It was the man who she'd kneed in the groin.

John rushed to her, lowered to her side and dragged her onto his lap. He unzipped her coat and ran his hands over her, inspecting her body for wounds. He squeezed his eyes shut, a half smile spreading across his mouth. "The vest caught the bullets." He hugged her. "You're going to be okay."

Her chest loosened enough from the viselike grip of agony for her to suck in a breath. She swallowed. Her throat felt swollen.

"Up," she whispered, her voice rough. "Help me up." She needed to be on her feet.

They had to move. There were too many men on the Delta team.

John grabbed the dead man's silenced weapon and something else from his utility belt before he hauled her up. "Eight fast-roped in. I don't know how many more came in by vehicle."

Were there a dozen of them tracking her? More? Why had they sent such a large team?

Leaning her against a tree, John gave her a second to catch her breath while he scanned the area.

"Come on," he said, taking two steps, and froze. "They're making a beeline toward my house." He gestured at the hill. "Head north. Around the lake to Asa's place." He was referring to one of the neighbors that didn't live too far away.

She shook her head. "I can't endanger anyone else."

"Go to the tree stand he uses for hunting. I'll make sure none of these bastards sneak up on your *six*," he said, using military jargon for *your back*, "and I'll meet you there."

"No, John." What was he thinking? He had no idea who these men were, what kind of hell she was up against. "You can't. It's too dangerous for you."

"Go." Ignoring her warning, he took off, darting around trees and disappeared like he was ready for full-on battle.

With the woods swarming with a large CIA hit squad, that was precisely what was going on tonight. Battle.

She grappled with the idea of following him for

the longest second of her life. Four key things she had learned about John were that he knew how to handle himself in a melee, never made a rash decision, never bit off more than he could chew and always demonstrated good judgment. Always.

Trusting him was best under the circumstances despite her concerns, because the truth of the matter was there wasn't time to dissuade him otherwise.

Shoving off the tree, she hurried toward the lake. She doggedly pushed ahead, gritting her teeth through the pangs in her chest. With the woods around her quiet, she tried to keep her sound signature to a minimum as she moved. Her heart pounded against her temples steady as a metronome while she cursed herself for getting John roped up in this deadly business. If anything happened to him, she'd never forgive herself.

At the perimeter, staying hidden in the tree line, she noticed a man from Delta team closing in from the north, sweeping the area headed in her direction. Her first instinct was to crouch down and wait for him to pass by and then take him out, but his attention swung her way and he spotted her.

Damn NVGs.

The man stiffened and leaped into action.

Full panic rolled through Zee. Going east wasn't an option. Most of the kill team were out that way and if she headed back in the direction from which she'd come, it would only endanger John more. Doubling back was a mistake.

That left her with one choice.

To go *across* the lake.

Gunfire split a branch not ten inches from her face, leaving her no chance to back out. She rallied and dashed forward.

John had warned her to stay off the lake in the winter. Even though it looked frozen solid, it wasn't meant to be an ice-skating rink. It was an accident tempting fate to happen.

The operative sprinted after her.

She ran for the lake, to the expanse of pristine landscape where moonlight glanced off spots of ice that showed through the white blanket of snow.

This was her only chance, without drawing more men toward John or falling into a trap.

If she steered clear of the center of the lake, staying close enough to the perimeter while remaining out of the range of gunfire, and if she had more luck than she preferred to count on, she might make it across.

Despite the hammering of her heart and the fear flooding her body, she stepped out onto the lake. Her feet slid a bit as she hit the ice, but she found her footing thanks to her thick-soled boots that provided traction.

There was a solid layer beneath her. Nothing shifted. It was probably safe. She kept moving and cast a quick look behind her.

The operative stepped out onto the lake, too, slipping and sliding on the icy surface, but determined to catch her, he followed without breaking his newfound stride.

She ran with caution, not wanting to wipe out in a nasty tumble, and listened for the slightest crack that could spell a watery demise.

Bullets peppered the ice, kicking up snow near her feet.

Whether the operative was aiming for her or the lake, the end result would soon be the same. Her dead.

To hell with caution. She bolted on a wing and a prayer and not much else.

Sweat rolled down her chest. Knees up high and pumping her arms, she gave it everything she had, leaving nothing in reserve.

But so did the man from Delta team. He took off like a hound from hell after her in hot pursuit.

Her bruised lungs were on fire. The air so crisp it was brittle. Each chilled breath scraped at her chest. She shot back at the man without looking. Anything to trip him up and knock him off-kilter.

Beneath the surface layer of powdery snow, the ice was slick, but she ran flat out, sliding and regaining her balance, all the while maintaining a forward trajectory.

She dared another glance over her shoulder.

He was only a few feet behind her. Gaining ground, shrinking the gap between them. Damn, he was close. And fast. He fired again.

She darted left and right. Her blood throbbed in her veins, her eyes burned with the cold, making tears stream down her face. She was almost to the other side. If she made it to the shore, she could lose him in the woods.

More bullets riddled the ground ahead of her.

The ice issued a gut-wrenching noise. *Crack!*

A sickening feeling gripped her heart.

Oh, no, no! She slowed, a foolish reflex to the

sound of impending doom, but she turned to take aim and eliminate the threat nipping at her heels.

In the distance, John had made it out onto the lake.

But the operative closing in, launched himself at her, propelling his body through the air. She shuffled backward, away, trying to get out of reach. He landed, taking her down with him.

Her teeth rattled in her head and her body shuddered, slamming against the hard surface.

The unmistakable sound of the world beneath them cracking and splitting rent the air. Her heart jumped into her throat. The frozen lake shifted with a groan.

Ice splintered, breaking. Water splashed to the surface.

She swung her weapon at his head, but too late. It was like the jaws of hell opened as the ice gave way.

"Zee!" She heard her name as she grasped at the slippery terrain, not finding any purchase. "Hold on!" John's voice was drawing closer, but he was still too far away.

Hurry, John.

The broken surface tipped, and the operative was sucked toward the black watery hole.

The man flailed wildly, trying desperately to grab hold of something, anything to stop his descent into the icy water. At the last second, he snatched on to her ankle, his fingers biting into her skin. She cried out as he dragged her along with him into the frigid depths.

Chapter Three

No!

Paralyzing horror tore through John at the sight of Zee being dragged into the water. At the sound of her bloodcurdling scream. He'd witnessed the all-too-brief struggle and watched in impotent fear as that coward had held fast to her leg in desperation and yanked her into the dark lake.

John ran like a man possessed, sliding as he went across the ice, moving as fast as he could with his bad leg and the slippery surface. He ignored the stabbing pain slicing down his right thigh, shooting to his shin. Moving on autopilot, he gave no thought to hauling enough air into his lungs, only to driving his body forward. Harder. Faster.

No time. There wasn't a moment to spare. With the combined weight of the man and the duffel on her back, she didn't stand a chance on her own. She was drowning, every air sac stretched to the limit ready to burst, fighting for her life under the water.

He had to get her. To save her. She wasn't going to die.

Not on his watch.

The surface of the lake was solid beneath him, but the closer he drew to the hole, fissures and growing slits spread, allowing water to rise. He didn't dare approach any farther upright or would risk becoming a victim himself.

He dropped to his belly and rolled the rest of the way, to distribute his body weight over a larger surface area, making the ice less likely to break more.

Nearing the edge of the hole, as close as he could get without the entire plane that he was on falling through, he prepared to shed his coat and dive in after her.

But Zee popped out of the water, gulping in oxygen. Her arms flailed as she still managed to hold on to her gun. She must've somehow shed the grasp of that man, shooting him, or kicking him loose.

Either way, she was downright amazing.

She went back under. For one excruciating moment his heart stopped. Then she bobbed up to the surface again. This time she swam to the edge of the hole and used her elbows to lift herself partially out of the water. Without a doubt she was strong, but the weight of her wet clothes and the pack would make it impossible for her to hoist herself out.

John unfastened his belt buckle and slid the leather strap free from his jeans. He tossed her the buckle end.

Zee caught the metal piece, sputtering up lake water, gasping for air. Still clutching her gun.

"Kick your legs. Try to get your whole body horizontal." John pulled her out as she kicked, holding on to the belt buckle. The muscles in his arms and back burned from the strain at the awkward angle. He tugged harder, dragging her from the watery hole and clear from the edge to safety.

Lying on her stomach, she rested, panting, and heaving up water.

More men in tactical gear, wearing NVGs and carrying suppressed weapons with laser sights, burst from the tree line and rushed out onto the ice.

They just kept coming, worse than a pack of insurgents with human resources to burn.

John took Zee by the elbow, ushering her on their knees along the ice farther away from the hole. Taking the duffel from her back, he helped her stand.

Without protest, she rushed for the shore. He shoved his hand in his coat pocket and withdrew the one item that he'd taken from the dead man's utility belt.

A fragmentation grenade.

He pulled the pin, cocked back his arm, and lobbed the explosive device high and far in the air. Without waiting for the explosion, he whirled and took off.

Once Zee reached the shore and made her way to a tree, he glanced back. The grenade hit the ice and skidded, sliding toward the assault team.

The men caught sight of it. They skittered, their arms windmilling, their boots sliding, trying frantically to alter their course. They did a sharp one-eighty in the opposite direction. But not all of them would make it.

John groaned through the pain in his leg, forced to hop and slow his pace. He set foot on land and looked back as the earsplitting sound erupted.

Boom!

Ice shattered, shooting up into the air in shards. The rest of the surface groaned and collapsed like a chain of dominoes falling. Two men yelped, the solid terrain beneath them dissolving, and they plummeted into the ice-cold water.

A secondary blast echoed in John's head as memories reared up, eclipsing him as if it were happening all over again.

Dust clogged the hot air. Rubble fell around his team. Shrapnel shredded his leg. The pain. The pain was unbearable. Immense pressure bore down on his chest. Debris had him pinned. But Dawes and Thomas were down.

"John!" The sound of his name pulled him from the flashback.

Frozen in place a second, he glanced around, dazed, reorienting himself. Snow-covered trees and the lake came into focus in a slow, sickening whirl.

Alaska. Not Syria.

Zee. They needed to run, to go. Now.

Across the lake, there was someone watching them.

One man wearing a trench coat over his black tactical gear, no NVGs, no helmet, stood on the shoreline with his hands in his pockets. Rather than showing a shred of concern for his drowning men or casting a glance at the ones who had survived the close call, he stared at John and Zee. Not as though he was in shock, but as if he had all the time in the world, and this was merely intermission.

It was the first time John had felt a twinge of fear facing an enemy. Or maybe it was only a symptom of his PTSD.

"John!" Zee called again.

He turned and rushed to her. She was bent over with hands on her knees, struggling to catch her breath.

"I called you five times," she said. "Did you hear me?"

Five?

Holy hell. He must've lost total awareness of what was happening around him. That was dangerous. That could get them both killed.

"I heard you." He put an arm around her and helped her through the woods, out of sight from the man in the trench coat. Their breath crystallized on the air in great white puffs as they hauled themselves through the snow. "Those men are going to come around the lake on foot." What was left of them anyway. "Change of plans. We're going to Old Man Bill's cabin."

"What?" She stared at him, shaking her head. "You told me never to go across his property. Isn't he crazy? Aren't there traps in the surrounding woods?"

"Old Man Bill is surly, not certifiable. But there are foothold traps and dangerous snares." To help him catch animals, not to hurt passersby who Bill felt should not be on his property to begin with. For that reason, there were numerous bright yellow no trespassing signs posted to the trees so no one would miss the warning. "The trick is to go from one tree with a sign to the next. I'll guide you since I know where his traps are, but I need to cover our trail in the snow as we go so those men don't track us. Move as quickly as you can. It'll be hard, but you've got to push yourself." After taking off his coat, he draped it around her. He estimated she'd be able to hustle for five to ten minutes before hypothermia and frostbite set in, overriding the adrenaline, and slowed her down.

Sweat slicked his brow and coated his back from all the exertion. Without a jacket he wouldn't last long either. The wind slashed right through his damp clothes. Already he could feel his body temperature dropping.

Shivering and dripping wet, she nodded, her teeth chattering from the cold.

He ached to get her warm. "Let's move out. Double time if you can."

They cut through the trees at a quick pace and when they reached the border of Old Man Bill's property, John directed her exactly how to move through the woods while he used a fallen pine bough to cover their tracks. The snow had picked up. A good thing on one hand. It would make it more difficult for the assault team to trail them. But the flip side of that was the snow and wind added to the misery of their tough trek up to the house, wearing them thin. It was so cold that John's lungs hurt every time he took a breath.

By the time they made it to Old Man Bill's cabin, Zee was in bad shape. Her lips were turning blue and the shiver had turned into an uncontrollable shake. He could only imagine what her feet were like, throbbing with fire until they went numb.

Shrugging the duffel from his shoulder, he dropped beside Bill's truck—a beater with a camper shell. John sat her down on top of the waterproof bag and leaned her against one of the tires. Tugging off his gloves, he looked her over more closely. Her eyelids looked heavy and her breathing was shallow.

"Stay with me. Okay?" He pulled one of his gloves on her hand, which was a block of ice, and had to pry the gun—a 9mm with an attached sound suppressor—from her other hand long enough to slip the second glove on. He gave her his knit hat as well to conserve her body heat, making sure to cover her ears. "Keep your eyes open and stay with me until I can get you warm." The sooner the better. They were only a hundred miles from the Arctic circle, and he estimated it was below zero tonight. The Alaskan elements were nothing to trifle with.

"We c-c-can't stay here."

"I know. Too close to the action. Trouble will soon close in." He rubbed his hands up and down her arms. "I'll get Bill to loan us his truck and get you out of here."

She nodded. "Cops. Have Bill…c-call cops." She wrapped her arms around her midsection, tremors racking through her, teeth chattering. "Their prime w-w-will hate—" she swallowed hard "—the interference."

Prime? What did that mean?

After the man in the woods had opened fire, shooting Zee twice without identifying himself, he was certain those guys weren't any kind of law enforcement. And if that assault team didn't want the cops, then that confirmed they weren't FBI or NSA. They could still be CIA, operating illegally on American soil. Or mercenaries. Or both.

"I'm sure the state troopers are already headed out to what's left of your house," he said, then he understood what she meant. The authorities would be out in droves, but in the wrong place. "You want Bill to have the police on this side of the lake." Where the assault team was headed.

She nodded, and in her eyes, he could see she was starting to fade.

"We could go to the police station," he said.

"They'll c-come for me." She shook her head. "Cops w-will die. Please, n-no."

Brutal men were hunting her, she was out here fighting for her life and she was worried about cops getting in the crosshairs?

Anger burned in his gut at thinking about how close she had come to death. "Wait here." He stood, stretching through the fiery ache coiling in his leg. John limped up to Bill's door, feeling the strain of the evening in every fiber of his being, and knocked. Before his neighbor opened up and thrust a gun in John's face, he identified himself. "Bill, it's John Lowry. From across the lake. I need assistance." After waiting a minute, he banged with his fist, repeating his words.

The porch light came on and the door cracked open. Bill peeked through over the chain on the door. He was close to ninety and had long white hair and a bushy white beard. "What in the hell, John? Do you have any idea what time it is?"

"Kill the light."

"Huh? What?"

"The light will attract unwanted attention." John crossed his arms, unable to fight off a shiver. "Kill it."

Bill's lips pinched and his mouth twisted like he was sucking on a lemon, but he turned off the bright porch light. "What do you want?"

"To borrow your truck for a few hours. Day at the most. Please don't ask questions I can't answer."

"Nope." Bill slammed the door.

Damn it. John listened for footfalls moving away. There were none. "I'll give you a hundred bucks." No response. "One thousand, Bill. It's an emergency. Life or death. If I didn't need your help, you know I wouldn't ask."

The chain slid off with a clink and the door opened again. Bill stood holding a shotgun in the crook of his elbow. "Let me see the money."

"I don't have it on me, but I'm good for it." The door swung to close, but John shoved his boot across the threshold, stopping it. "I give you my word as a man of honor."

"Honor won't put food on my table or bourbon in my gut. Know what I'm saying?"

John looked at his watch. His gaze fell across the stainless-steel case, the black ceramic bezel, the strap made from sturdy canvas sail. He unfastened it and took off the watch. "This is a Blancpain Fifty Fathoms. It's worth seven grand. More than your ride. I get it back when you get your truck and the cash. Deal?" He handed over his most prized possession. Not that he cared about luxury items, but his SEAL team had all chipped in for this parting gift, the officers coughing up more than the enlisted. The inscription meant more to him than the watch itself.

"I can't tell the difference between a blank pan and any other froufrou watch." Bill snatched the priceless timepiece from his hand and inspected it. "It sure does look expensive. All right. I believe you. But in the back of the truck, I've got wood I chopped down out at Salcha," he said, referring to the salvage woodlot. "I want it all returned."

John restrained a sigh. "No problem."

"And for you to unload it for me?" Bill asked, and John nodded, willing to help his elderly neighbor with the task under any circumstances. "The keys are in the truck. In the visor."

"One more thing. Call the police. Tell them you saw suspicious men in the woods. Tactical gear and laser sights. Not a word to anyone about me." He was glad he'd had the foresight to keep Zee hidden on the other side of the truck. The less Bill knew, the better. "Got it?"

He didn't expect much pushback from Bill or questions for that matter. People out here tended to mind their own business.

Bill eyed him long and hard. Then he gave a two-finger salute. "Tallyho." The door slammed shut.

John hurried down the steps to the truck.

Scanning the area for movement, he opened the driver's door. The woods were quiet, and the coast was clear. For now. But not for much longer.

They needed to get on the road before that assault team was in the chopper and searching from the sky. At this hour, they'd be easy to spot. With any luck, those boys still had boots on the ground and were combing the area on foot.

John slipped his hands under Zee's arms, hauled her up and got her into the truck. Grabbing hold of the bag, he glanced around once more, his gaze searching for any sign of a threat before he climbed in and set the duffel in the back on top the firewood.

Flipping down the visor, he found the keys as they plopped into his palm. He cranked the engine, keeping the headlights off, and turned on the heat. "It'll take a minute to warm up."

HE SWUNG OUT onto the road, following it until they hit Elliott Highway, which was part of Route 2. On the main road, he turned on the headlights to avoid getting pulled over by the state troopers.

Once the heater got going, he put it on full blast to chase away the cold. Little good it seemed to do. Zee was shaking harder and slipping faster.

"You hanging in there?" he asked, his own tremors setting in from the exposed cold with his clothing damp from sweat.

"Y-yeah."

"Sing something. It'll help your mind focus. Keep you alert." It would also cue him in to the state of her condition, whether she was improving or worsening. "Pick anything. Though I'm partial to country."

She gave a shallow half laugh as her mouth quirked. Through her rattling teeth, she started singing.

He had expected her to pick a pop song, but the lyrics to "The Ants Go Marching" spilled from her lips. The choice of a nursery rhyme was surprising.

Not as shocking as the covert op that had un-raveled in his backyard or how this entire time she hadn't let go of her gun. She clung to the weapon like a lifeline. The practiced way someone of his ilk would, knowing that a gun was as essential to sur-vival as food and shelter.

In so many ways, he would've sworn that he knew Zee. What made her tick, made her smile, made her angry. Her favorite color and dessert. That she valued hard work. Never tried to skate by on her sensational looks. All about her childhood growing up feeling like she didn't belong in Breezy Point—what Zee had described as the least diverse and most insular right-wing area in New York City—with a Black demo-crat mom and a republican Irish dad. How she came from a family of cops and was a patriot who under-stood that sometimes self-sacrifice for the greater good was necessary.

John could distinguish her laugh from a hundred others blindfolded.

But he didn't even know her last name. Or the real reason she was hiding out in Alaska. She had first introduced herself as Zoey—*just call me Zee*—like she was Cher, Madonna, Beyoncé. He'd thought it cute at the time. Then those perimeter alarms went up. That combined with her initial hesitancy to be around him for long periods of time, especially alone together indoors—and when they were, she had al-ways been armed—had him chalking it up to a luna-tic ex. Women moved and changed their identities to get away from an abusive ex-husband far more than they should have to.

She had seemed to need a friend who could keep his distance and not push. So he'd been that for her.

Who are you, Zee? What are you hiding and what kind of trouble are you in? How deep does it go?

He'd get answers, one way or another. No more evasion. No more secrets permissible. But now wasn't the time to grill her. Once she was safe and warm, he'd demand the truth.

Zee's lyrics began to slow and slur. "H-h-hurrah," she sang barely above a whisper, "...hur..." Her head lolled to the side as she slumped down in the seat and the gun slipped from hand, clattering to the foot well.

John slammed on the accelerator, gunning the engine. "Zee!" He shook her. "Wake up. Don't fall asleep."

They weren't far. He cut off the highway, turning down the road toward the campground, the rear end of the truck fishtailing.

No CCTV in the vicinity to give away their position and there were public recreational cabins. They were located along trails and near remote lakes in backcountry areas such as this. State park staff did their best to keep the cabins tidy between uses. You were supposed to reserve one, but he doubted anybody would be out here this close to Christmas.

Two miles down the road he came to a cabin. No vehicles were parked nearby, and no one went hiking this time of year.

He cut the engine and eyed her bag. Whatever was in it, he was certain there'd be critical provisions. Snatching the duffel, he hurried from the truck inside the cabin for a quick once-over. It was empty. A simple single room in decent condition. He dropped the bag and hightailed it back to the truck.

Opening her door, he caught her before she fell out. He pushed her wet hair from her face, took her gun and scooped her into his arms. With his bad leg, he kicked the door closed, balancing on his good one. Despite his injury, perhaps because of it, he worked on maintaining the honed strength of his body, particularly in the muscles that supported his knees, with weight-bearing exercises. His diligent efforts paid off, enabling him to hustle up the steps, carrying her, and whisk her inside without faltering.

She was so cold and wet. The feel of her body sent a chill shooting down his spine.

He set her down on the wood floor. Took a quick inventory of her bag for something to help them. Bundles of cash—at least twenty thousand, prepaid VISA cards, sleeping bag, MREs—meals ready to eat. Change of clothes, passport and IDs for a Zadie Hall and Zoey Howard, which he doubted either was her real name, medical kit, fire starter packets, laptop, burner phone *and* a sat phone. Not something you see every day.

The cabin had a wood-burning stove and getting Zee warm was his number-one priority. He dashed back to the truck and grabbed some logs. Bill wouldn't miss a few pieces. Then again, he might, but the money his neighbor was going to receive was more than adequate compensation.

John made swift work of building a fire that would last a few hours and rolled out a Hyperion sleeping bag. A solid choice, it was ultralightweight and extremely warm, but the fastest way to raise her body temperature was skin on skin.

She might be livid enough to slap him later, but at least she'd be alive to do it, and that was the only thing that mattered to him. Zee living to see another day.

Taking a deep breath, he started with her boots and worked his way up. John had imagined undressing her a hundred times, but never under such dire circumstances. Thinking about it, the fantasy had entailed them taking off each other's clothes. A mutual act of consent and desire. Welcomed affection.

Not like this.

Averting his eyes, he treated her as he would any battle brother, sister in arms, who needed him. He laid her in the sleeping bag close to the fire and covered her. With his back to her, he stripped down to his birthday suit, desperate to drive away the terrible cold in his own limbs.

Quickly, he strung a nylon cord he found in her bag and hung their clothes near the fire.

He grabbed the gun, keeping it close, and climbed in alongside her. Her skin was cold and clammy, her body stiff.

What was the protocol? Roll her away from him with her back to his front? But if he put his arms around her, he might accidentally touch an intimate body part.

There wasn't enough room in the sleeping bag for them to lie back-to-back.

This was a KISS situation. *Keep it simple, stupid.*

Staying as they were, front to front with her back to the fire, he brought his body closer, zipped them up in the down-filled cocoon, and curled his arms around her.

John had full control over his mind and in turn over his body. In truth, he refused to allow himself to enjoy being close to her beyond the much-needed heat they generated together. With the cold and exhaustion dampening any appreciation for the moment, it wasn't too hard.

But he feared warming up and falling asleep for two reasons.

First, they might be found, caught off guard.

Second, if he allowed his mind to relax, his body would follow, relinquishing control to Mother Nature. The last thing he wanted was for her to come to and find his lower appendage standing at attention while he slept.

There was only one thing he could do. Even though his leg was hurting, and he was in bad need of shut-eye, he vowed not to sleep.

After a few minutes, her head inclined forward, resting on his chest, and she nestled against him. They both stopped shaking not long after, settling into the sleeping bag. Relief trickled through his heart. Hypothermia and shock would not take her from him tonight. A little bloom of contentment unfolded inside him as he held her tighter.

With rest, she would be all right. And that brought him more comfort and peace of mind than eight hours of sleep ever would.

Chapter Four

Zee jerked awake, her sluggish mind swimming, her fists clenched ready to fight, her heavy eyelids refusing to lift. What happened? Where was she? Where was Delta team?

"Shh." A soothing male voice in her ear. "I've got you. I won't let anything happen to you. I swear it."

John.

If she was with John, she was safe. She relaxed into the soft warmth of skin against skin.

Gentle fingers pushed hair from her face and tested the pulse at her throat. Strong arms surrounded her, enfolding her in sublime heat. Zee pressed her face to his bare chest. Inhaled the scent of testosterone and fire smoke. She curled an arm around his waist, tucked a leg between his and let the undertow of exhaustion pull her back to sleep.

Sometime later—an hour, several, she didn't know—she opened her eyes to the smell of coffee. She was in a cabin. In a sleeping bag, alone and naked.

Memories rushed back on a tide of fear in her foggy brain, ticking up her heartbeat. The assault on her cabin. The explosion. John's help in the woods. Taking two bullets to protect him, which explained the soreness in her chest.

The lake. Getting dragged into the icy water.

Utter terror. She had thrashed and had fought. Shot the man holding her and had kicked and kicked until she was free of his grasp. Pain, searing and hot, had cut through her chest. But she had to reach the surface. Swam through the darkness, pushed against the cold and the heaviness of the duffel on her back, her wet clothes. Then air. And John had pulled her out of the water.

Lightheaded, soaked, freezing they had made it to Bill's house. Then she didn't remember much else.

Except for John. The sound of his voice as he had spoken to her. Snuggled beside him, as close together as a man and woman could be without having sex. The steady thrum of his heartbeat. The precious warmth of his skin against hers. The intimate feel of him. *All of him.* Chiseled muscle of his chest. Sculpted abdomen. Hair on his hard thighs and between his legs. The length of him pressed to her belly.

A different kind of heat slid through her. The kind that had her aching to have him back in the sleeping bag with her.

"John?" She pushed up on her forearm and a wave of dizziness slowed her.

"Take it easy." He knelt in front of her, fully dressed, and helped her sit up while keeping her covered.

"What time is it?" Her internal clock was kaput

and in December, they got less than four hours of daylight, starting around eleven.

"About eight in the morning. Here." He handed her coffee in one of the collapsible mugs from her duffel. "I was able to heat some water on the stove in the small titanium pot you packed. Good thing you had water-purifying tablets. You thought of pretty much everything, though a foil blanket and hand warmers would've been good. I didn't eat the MRE. I saved it for you, but I did have some of the coffee."

She took the mug and sipped. Bitter warmth slid down her throat to her stomach, spreading through her. "You should eat. There are a thousand calories in one of those meals. Just save me the cheese and crackers." She had two more MREs and could share one.

He gave her a lopsided grin and heart skipped a beat.

Lifting his hand to her face, he brushed her jaw with his knuckles, sending a tingle from her cheek to her toes. Time came to a halt as they stayed like that. There was nothing but the two of them for a moment. His green eyes held hers and his face softened as the air backed up in her lungs.

She liked the way he looked at her and she loved the way he made her feel.

At ease. Safe.

Yes, both of those beautiful things just looking in his eyes.

"I guess I'll address the elephant in the room," he said, lowering his gaze and hand. "Sorry I undressed you without your permission. You were unconscious and hypothermic. You could've died. I didn't take advantage of the situation in any manner." He spoke in a rush, as if he were nervous, but she'd never seen John nervous.

She believed him. The circumstances had been grave. They both could've died. Most men would've ogled, some might've copped a feel, others could've done worse, but John was not most men.

"It was to preserve body heat only," he continued, "and keep you alive. Nothing inappropriate happened. Promise. I just couldn't let—"

Unable to stop herself, she slipped a hand around the nape of his neck, sliding her fingers in his hair, and brought his mouth to hers. She had wanted to know, wanted to feel him. Taste him. For so long.

His arms went around her as his warm firm lips moved over hers, brushing, seeking, and she moaned at the feel of his hot tongue. He held her close and tight, like he had craved this, too.

The kiss sizzled through her, slow and sensuous, drowning her in sensation. Heat slid through her, racing under her skin. She leaned in to him, her body igniting under the edgy delight.

She wanted more. To haul him down to the sleeping bag, strip off his clothes and make love to him, right here in this austere cabin on the wooden floor.

But she'd endangered him far too much already, and she refused to drag him in to her mess any deeper.

A sudden, heartrending thought occurred to her. This beautiful, toe-curling kiss was their first. And it had to be their last.

The only way to protect him was to let him go.

Ignoring the hot throb between her legs and the achy tension coiling low in her belly, she tore her mouth away with a knot forming in her chest. "Thank you, for helping me. For saving my life."

Their gazes met. It was almost as if she saw straight into his soul, and the powerful sense of connection to him was overwhelming.

"You're welcome." He moved in to kiss her again, but she pulled back.

A deep ache bled into a deeper longing and if it had only been physical between them, she would've given in.

Lowering her head, she said, "I'm grateful, John. But that's all." A horrible lie, but a necessary one. "The kiss was a gesture of appreciation to show you that undressing me was no big deal between good friends."

He sank back on his heels and the expression dawning on his face sent a pang shooting through her chest. "Oh. I thought…"

"You should go," she said, swallowing a scream of yearning and sorrow and anger.

"Go?"

"Can you pass me my clothes?" She shifted, putting her back to him. "I need to get dressed."

"Right." He handed her the clothes that he had hung up near the stove. "Your boots should be good to go. I removed the soles and put heated rocks inside them, so they'd dry quickly. I'll wait outside while you dress, then we can talk."

"There's nothing to discuss. When I said you should go, I meant you should leave."

"Leave? What are you talking about?"

She unzipped the sleeping bag to climb out.

Averting his gaze, he spun around and faced the door.

She stabbed her legs into her jeans and yanked them up over her hips. It wasn't until her socks and sweater were on that she realized she'd been in such a rush last night that she'd forgotten underwear. There was some in her duffel, but no time for it now. She had to rip off this Band-Aid between her and John. Send him on his way.

"I'm talking about how you need to let a sense of self-preservation override chivalry and take off," she said.

"Take off? What about you?"

She tugged on warm boots and laced them up. Neat trick with the rocks. "Why do you keep repeating everything I say?"

Sighing, he scrubbed a hand over his face. "Are you dressed?"

She considered lying, but she couldn't pretend she was naked for the duration of this conversation. Perhaps she should have delayed putting on clothes. "I am."

He whirled around. The confusion on his face had been replaced with a grimace. "What's your real name?"

She hesitated.

"Don't lie to me," he warned. "If you do, I'll know."

"Zenobia. Hanley."

"Zenobia," he repeated as if trying it out on his tongue. "Why are those men after you? Who are they? FBI? NSA black ops? The mob? I would've guessed CIA since I've worked with enough of those guys to know how they move, but they can't operate on American soil."

"Stop asking questions."

"I deserve answers." He crossed his arms over his chest. "I've earned the right. Start talking."

She drew in a shaky breath. "The answers will only get you killed."

"So be it."

Incredible. This man would not back down. "I'm not a criminal, but I am on the run."

"Good start. Go on."

"The rest is classified."

He put his hands on his hips, standing his ground. "Then give me the redacted version."

She growled in frustration. He was stubborn as a mule.

The nature of her trouble *was* classified and telling him too much would open Pandora's box in his life. She was a former CIA operative, trained to withstand interrogation, but he wasn't going to accept her stonewalling. Fierce determination blazed in his steely eyes.

The heat of his stare was scorching, and inside this operative's skin, the woman was melting. She had to tell him something. A nugget of truth, small enough for him to swallow and large enough to scare him off.

"You're a movie buff," she said. "Did you ever see *The Warriors*?"

He folded his arms again, his eyes narrowing, and his jaw clenched. "No."

"They were a mixed-race street gang in 1970s New York City. They were blamed for a murder they didn't commit. Caught uptown in enemy territory, they had to make their way back home to Coney Island with all the other gangs gunning for them. So they ran. Or rather they fought and ran. Until they could prove their innocence. My former team—think of us as the Warriors. Only we did kill someone, under orders, but it turned out to be the wrong person. The op was bad from the beginning. I couldn't put my finger on it, but I didn't have a good feeling about that one and then everything went sideways. Before we could get answers from our handler, all the other gangs came for us. Anyone we get close to is in danger. Understand?"

Oddly, John nodded as if he understood completely. He paced the length of the cabin, rubbing his chin. Digesting that nugget of truth.

"They don't know who you are. Yet," she said. "Let's keep it that way. You need to leave."

"How do you think they found you?" he asked, still moving from one end of the room to the other.

"On my recent trips to Fairbanks, I started digging around to find evidence to clear our names. Breached their database. I was careful, but I must've stayed online too long that last time. Hackers, we leave behind virtual fingerprints in an intrusion— a preference for a particular type of tool or action, typos in a command line, the nature of the activity itself. Everything can be masked with enough caution and preparation, except for the last item." The nature of the activity. No one else would hack into the specific CIA database she had breached, and certainly not into the file labeled Topaz. "I guess I didn't get out of the system before an alarm had been tripped or an analyst had noticed."

He stopped and looked up at her; his eyes were unreadable, but he didn't appear the slightest bit daunted. "Have you seen *The Godfather*?"

She wasn't sure where he was going with this, but she didn't think she'd like it. "Who hasn't?"

"You have to go to the mattresses," he said matter-of-factly.

Now she was the one confused. "I understand the phrase means go to war."

"But do you know why they call it that?"

"They never explained the mattresses part in the movie."

"It's because the mob family had to move out of their home and hole up someplace where no one could find them and all their soldiers. But they had to do it quickly, so that they could get the jump on the rival family. They had places stashed around the city with the mattresses on the floor. And that's where they would make their stand until they nailed the boss of the rival family. You're not at war right now, you're on the run," he said, and it was as though she was seeing him clearly for the first time—a battle-hardened warrior unafraid to rush back into the fray. "You need to stop running and make a stand. But you need men. You need me." He flashed that grin at her and tucked his tongue in his cheek.

How in the hell had he turned this around?

He was too smart for his own good.

"No," she said, waving her hands to emphasize her point. "You need to get out of here." She stabbed a finger in his direction.

He stared down at her, rooted firmly in place. "I'm not going anywhere without you," he said, his tone adamant.

"But you are. Please, leave."

"Some of those men were headed in the direction of my place last night. They probably already know who I am."

"They have no reason to come after you unless you're with me, but it's best that you don't go home for a few days."

Concern etched his face, but she suspected that none of it was for himself.

"The Warriors, did they win in the end?" he asked.

"Yeah. They did."

"How?" He leaned against the wall, his expression intense, his full attention lasered on her. "Did they do it alone while scattered, or together working as a team?"

Zee folded her arms and gritted her teeth at how he was twisting things around on her. "I can't turn to the rest of my team." They were all in hiding, supposedly off the grid, and she didn't know where.

Glancing at her duffel bag, she thought about the SAT phone inside. It was meant for a one-time, dire-straits call to her former team leader Hunter Wright. But using the phone now wouldn't solve her immediate problem.

"All the more reason you need me. You can't do this alone," John said, and she hated the bite of truth in his words. "I take it you're going to try to get out of Alaska. Head back to the lower forty-eight."

She looked at him with an annoyed frown over the fact that he was right. "What makes you think that?"

"You hate it up here in the freezing wilderness. You'll want to go someplace you can navigate easier on your own."

He was half right.

John lifted a brow, pleased with himself. "I can help you get out of Alaska under the radar. Fast."

The one thing she didn't have was an impromptu exit strategy out of this state that was two and a half times the size of Texas. Her original plan had been to lie low in a state park if a team had ever showed up to take her out. But that was before she'd left her laptop behind. With the area crawling with operatives and not knowing if they had her computer, she had to get to Seattle before that assault team figured out why she would head there.

Time was of the essence and she had no clue what her next move was.

Thanks to John having done a brilliant job illustrating why she needed him, her annoyance with him ballooned; all the while her fear of him getting hurt or worse on her behalf swelled in her chest, making it hard to breathe.

He wouldn't listen to reason, so she used a different tactic.

She stormed across the room to the door and flung it open. "Take off for a week. Go on a vacation. Enjoy your retirement."

His eyes flashed, their bright green color turning a hard malachite, and he looked as though he'd been slapped. "Enjoy my retirement? Is that a sick joke?"

Whoa. That had struck a nerve. One that she hadn't anticipated.

Zee was stunned by his reaction. John was well, she had no idea how old he was exactly. Somewhere between forty and fifty, she guessed. Not that he looked that old. In fact, he was strong and vital, might not even be forty yet. It was the way he carried himself, with a seen-it-all manner, and spoke about things. Like a wise, old soul.

But she hadn't meant senior-citizen type of retirement.

John marched up to her and slammed the door shut. "You're facing a formidable force and you're not going to win this war by yourself."

She had serious skills cultivated over the years, but she was far from being an army of one.

Through the havoc of her feelings, she said, "I'm just trying to survive the battle for now." She blew out a heavy breath. "You've already gotten in too deep and for that, I'm sorry." More than he would ever know. "But it's not too late for you. Go home."

"I have nothing waiting for me back home, and I've got nothing left to lose...besides you."

Her heart clenched violently. What was he saying? What did it mean?

He cupped her face in both of his hands. His thumbs stroked her cheeks in a tender, sweeping caress that made her chest ache. "I want to protect you, Zee." His unwavering gaze was an anchor weighing down her heart. "Let me."

Want. She shivered at the word, the chill running both hot and cold. After what he'd already gone through last night, he still wanted to protect her.

"You have your life, John. I'd like you to keep it." When he looked at her like that, touched her, it was hard to think. Impossible to refuse him anything. *Please, please, go.* Otherwise, she was going to have to do something awful. Say something to hurt him, to save him. She would hate herself for it, but if it meant he'd never become collateral damage, then the pain would be worth it. "Now, stay the hell away from me."

Doing the exact opposite, John edged closer, bringing them chest to chest, and rubbed her arms. "Listen to me and stop being so stubborn," he said, his smooth, deep voice dipping in a way that curled in her belly. "Let me help you."

It was all too much and took everything in her not to lean against his solid frame, absorb his warmth, accept his help, rely on his comfort.

John was steadfast, reliable and she needed his help. So much was at stake, not just her own life, and she wanted him at her side, as more than a hired gun or a friend.

But what would it cost him?

No, this wasn't fair to him. He deserved better than getting further embroiled in her trouble.

Zee turned her back to him. If she looked him in the eye, she wouldn't be able to go through with it and force him to leave. An emotional attack was the logical choice.

He stepped up behind her and curled his hands around her shoulders, sending a tingle across her nerves that almost stopped her. Almost.

"I don't need you," she said. "Don't want you around." Her eyes stung as she tried to breathe. "You were great, doing my hunting and chopping my firewood, but beyond that what good are you to me? I don't want the dead weight of a disabled retiree slowing me down. I already took two bullets for you." Was that her voice cracking? She needed to hold it together, stay firm and lie to John for his own sake. She drew in a sharp breath against a pain more shocking than she wanted it to be. "I can find some other sucker to get me out of Alaska."

The security of his warm hands slipped away from her arms. The heavy thud of boots stomped across the room. Keys jangled. The door opened and slammed closed.

The world went watery, but she refused to let the tears welling in her eyes fall as her heart broke into pieces.

Chapter Five

Speeding away from the cabin headed down the snow-covered road, John cursed himself for a fool.

Damn her, and damn himself for letting her breach the wall he'd built up over the past three years and for getting so caught up in her that he couldn't think straight.

His brain was twisted into such a pretzel that when she had kissed him, he had actually thought it had been real. That it had meant to her what it had to him.

A heck of a lot more than a mere gesture between good friends.

The word *friends* had slapped his heart as though she'd let loose a taut rubber band against it.

Last night, the intimacy of lying beside her had been staggering. Their breaths mingled, with him smelling the heat of her skin, feeling the solid thumps of her heart beating.

Before his injury and his discharge from the service, women had been easy come, easy go. No risk of an emotional connection. No one worth holding on to. The mission had always been his top priority.

The SEAL teams came first, and he had given them everything he had. He'd seen too many broken relationships with his battle brothers to put any real effort into one.

What would've been the point? A bitter divorce? Loss of half his military pension? Kids who didn't understand why he had to drop everything and leave whenever the call came and ended up hating him for it?

But with Zee, when they spent time together, he didn't feel alone. Not once in his life could he say that about any other woman. Slowly, he had let her into his heart, had shown her his vulnerabilities, and in turn had given her the power to eviscerate him with a few choice words.

The muscles in John's shoulders bunched and tightened like cords of thick rope that had swollen and shrunken. He was shaking with anger. Not only for the things she'd said to him, but also for what she was going through and for not being able to convince her to put him to good use instead of putting him out to pasture, the same as the military.

His abrupt discharge from the service had been less jarring than the way she'd booted him from the cabin. He couldn't remember ever being so angry—most of all at himself.

He was the biggest idiot. Had risked his life for her last night and had been prepared to do it again, to put it all on the line for her, a woman whose real name he had just learned.

He believed her story about her op going wrong and needing to prove her innocence. Whatever system she'd breached, his guess was the CIA's, it had scared someone enough to send a large team of commandos to eliminate one woman. He had experienced firsthand precisely what she was up against, the magnitude of her problem, but it would take a little more than that to scare him off.

One of those operators had gotten the drop on him and Zee had saved his life. When she'd lunged in front of him and taken those bullets, it had been like all the oxygen had been sucked out of the atmosphere and then he'd flown into a rage and killed the man who had shot her.

They had saved each other, working together. As a team.

But she'd never spoken to him the way she had in the cabin, not in the nine months they'd known each other. He didn't think she was capable of such… flagrant disrespect. Of wounding him so viciously.

Disabled retiree!

The deep blow of those two words had struck him even harder than *friends*. Putting an end to the discussion.

What more could he have said to her?

Technically, he was disabled according to Veterans Affairs with a ninety percent combined rating for his leg and PTSD. And yes, technically, he was retired from the military. But it was *the way* she had said it.

The same way he felt at times, sitting cooped up in his cabin with his memories for company, like he was useless. Worthless.

Except when he was with her, especially last

night. He had been his old self. A little slower, but no less effective.

How dare she speak to him in that manner after everything he'd done for her?

Not that she owed him anything for the help he'd freely given, other than the respect he had earned.

Her cruel words rang in his head, taunting him. *Sucker. Disabled. Retiree.* The sting burned through him all over again.

He'd show her who was a disabled retiree. It wasn't him. He was still a force to be reckoned with.

John stomped on the brakes, slapped the steering wheel and cranked it, whipping the truck around.

Galvanized by what she thought of him, he raced back to the cabin and threw the truck in Park with the engine running. It took him less than ten seconds to clear the vehicle and burst through the door.

Zee whirled around, those gorgeous brown eyes narrowing for a fight, the gun in her hand pointed at his head. As always, the sight of her gave him a quick inner jolt, the sheer beauty of her stealing his breath. Her face should be captured in an oil painting. It would rival the *Mona Lisa*, or the *Girl with a Pearl Earring* and he'd call it *Goddess with a Gun*.

She had a face that men would kill for.

Hell, he already had and might very well again.

Zee lowered the weapon. "What on earth are you doing back here?"

A part of him was asking himself the same question, but in his gut, he knew this was where he needed to be. His internal compass had never led him astray.

"I may be disabled but I'm not an invalid," John said, coolly, despite the fact he was livid. He had never raised his voice to her and never would. "I was forced into retirement but there's still plenty of fight left in me. You did take two bullets for me and by the way don't ever do that again. But I'm the one who warned you about the strike team approaching."

"And I appreciate the heads-up, but—"

"Nope." He raised a hand to silence her as he cut her off. "I'm not finished speaking." It required every bit of his strength to keep his voice even. "I stopped one of those men from apprehending you in the woods. Prevented you from drowning by dragging you out of the freezing lake. Kept that team from following you. Brought you to safety and I made sure you didn't die from hypothermia while remaining a perfect gentleman." Which had nearly been an impossible feat. He was learning that he could do what was required when it came to her. Even set aside his anger and bruised feelings to do the right thing. "In short, you would be dead if not for me. Why don't you tally up the scorecard before you start hurling any more insults?"

Her mouth dropped open as she rocked back on her heels.

"You may not want my help, but you need it." He charged inside, grabbed her duffel with one hand and Zee's elbow with the other, fully aware this woman knew how to handle herself and if given the chance could very well take him down in a few moves. "That's a fact, plain and simple. You're too smart not to see that."

As he hauled her and the bag to the truck, his words sank in. She was too smart. He recalled how she always managed to beat him at chess, strategized, willing to sacrifice her queen and any other player. It was foolish of her not to use him, and she was no fool.

So, why had she discarded him faster than a used tissue?

"When you were sleeping this morning," he said, "I swore to protect you. Not to let anything happen to you. That's a promise I intend to keep whether you like it or not." He opened the passenger's door, steered her inside to sit, dumped the bag on her lap and closed the door.

Hustling around the front of the truck, he decided then and there not to be dissuaded by anything ugly she might say. He'd get her out of Alaska and settled someplace safe. Where he wouldn't worry about her, wondering if she was dead or alive. Regardless of whether she only saw him as a friend and had no real feelings for him, it didn't change the fact that he had a heart full for her.

If anything happened to her when he had the power to prevent it, it would wreck him. The kind of devastation one didn't get over.

He hopped in the truck.

She stared at him in wide-eyed disbelief.

"I let you draw the line between us, Zee, and now I'm moving it," he said. "You can poke holes in me if you want, try to turn me into Swiss cheese to see how much I can take, and we can waste time arguing, all of which would only work in that assault team's favor. I suggest instead you tell me where you want to go, I'll help you get there, ensure you're safe and off their radar. Then since you want me gone so badly, I'll walk away like you want. No strings attached. Just tell me where you want to go."

Imposing his will on others wasn't his usual style. Taking this approach with her sickened him, but her plan was suicidal. He simply couldn't abide it.

The fire in her eyes dimmed as her rigid posture relaxed in acquiescence, and a tingle of relief loosened the fist clenching his heart.

She clutched the bag to her heaving chest. "Seattle," she said, her voice low and soft.

John tensed. *A large city.*

Reflexively, he checked his coat pockets, but he knew he'd left his meds back at the cabin. Going to Fairbanks was a struggle for him while medicated and Seattle had more than twenty times the size of that population. The last time he had taken his pills was…two days ago since he'd felt good. No, better than good, great. Sometimes he skipped whole days because his routine was working. Every day he'd been taking long, strenuous walks when the sun was up for endorphins, and he'd been spending loads more time with Zee, which had always been a pleasure, alleviating any stress. But now he was forty-eight hours without any medication in his system and the pressure was going to continue to build.

You'll be fine. You just need some sleep.

Zee shifted toward the window and dabbed at the corners of her eyes like she was the aggrieved party. "I need to get there today. As soon as possible. Then we can go our separate ways, and you stay away from me."

The word *need* struck him along with the urgency to make it happen. He ruled out driving there and flying commercial, but he had an idea that might take some finagling to work.

He put the truck in Drive and hit the accelerator. Tamping down his emotions, he buried them deep in the same manner he used to before he went on an op.

"John, tell me exactly what you used to do in the military that gives you the unflappable confidence to help me."

It wasn't confidence and it wasn't chivalry and certainly wasn't unflappable. He was crazy about her. Another fact that was cut-and-dried. But he would spill the details of his professional background as she demanded.

"I'll explain on the way to Bill's," he said, planning not to hold anything back from her. Not so much to impress her, although he wouldn't mind if that was a byproduct, but to remind himself what he was capable of and who he was deep down at his core. "We'll need him to drop us off somewhere." And since John wouldn't be back in twenty-four hours, he didn't want to give the old guy an excuse to keep his watch.

Chapter Six

Six men down and nothing to show for it. Ryker clenched his jaw, wanting to tear something or someone apart. State troopers had fanned out in the woods surrounding the lake, putting a premature end to Delta team's search.

Ryker didn't have a single lead on where Zenobia was now.

It seemed so long ago when he had first approached Zee and asked her out while she was living in Germany. The most challenging aspect of cultivating a relationship with her had been pretending to be a normal person. Killing had always been easy for him. Making conversation with a beautiful young woman, coming on strong without being overly aggressive had been much harder. To pull it off, he had imagined himself a magician playing a shell game. Instead of hiding an object and shuffling around cups, the trick had been to keep her from seeing the true nature of his character.

He had been very good at it. For a while. And for as long as he had maintained that psychoemotional sleight of hand they had enjoyed their time together.

If only he hadn't gotten complacent and given up the charade. Had figured out how to juggle being Jekyll for her and Hyde the rest of the time without her ever knowing the truth.

If he had, where would they be today?

Delta Two entered from the adjoining room.

"What have you found?" Ryker asked his second-in-command.

They had rented two connecting rooms at the inn on Eielson Air Force Base, twenty-five minutes from Fairbanks, where they were regrouping while the helicopter was refueled.

"We combed through the neighbor's place. The man helping her is John Lowry. He's a retired master chief special warfare operator. Was assigned to SEAL Team Two."

Ryker stiffened, the tidbit giving him pause for a moment, but it made sense. The man who had gotten Zee out of the lake and thrown the grenade was a skilled operator. Ryker had recognized that immediately. But a SEAL?

"I got you the unredacted file on him." Two handed over the tablet to Ryker. "A real die-hard hotshot. Knows how to dig in for a fight. More medals than me and Five combined. There's nothing this guy hasn't done. Direct action raids. Rounding up and eliminating high-value targets. Sensitive-site exploitation to collect information. Thrown himself in harm's way to protect his guys. Been a prisoner of war and tortured."

"Was he also single-handedly responsible for killing Osama bin Laden?" Ryker asked sarcastically.

"That was SEAL Team Six," his guy said, and Ryker rolled his eyes. "But Lowry is still impressive. We'll need to take extra precautions."

Ryker tuned out his second-in-command gushing over Lowry. As he read the former SEAL's résumé, his blood pressure skyrocketed and all he saw was red.

For years, Ryker had been itching to hurt Zee the way she had hurt him. To make her pay for her betrayal. Finally, the CIA had cut her loose, depriving her of their protection. She was on the run, without her team or Hunter Wright to fall back on for assistance—*his for the taking*—and she had somehow managed to ingratiate herself to the one man in the local area who was a fire-seasoned killing machine.

He burned with raw hatred for that ungrateful, lucky bitch. Surely she was sleeping with the former SEAL, had exerted her witchlike wiles on him and seduced him into helping her. Images flashed through his head of Zenobia curled up in bed with this man, Lowry. Touching him. Kissing him. Making love to him.

Ryker growled his frustration. He flipped over the table, smashed the tablet under his foot and swept everything from the dresser to the floor.

Two eased back, clearing out into the next room with the others.

Giving one last howl of rage, a veritable blood cry, he expelled the pressure building in his chest. Lowry deserved to die for getting close to her, sleeping with her. They both did and would know his wrath as soon as he found them.

Ryker went to the mirror. Slicked back his blond hair that had fallen out of place. He held on to the fury simmering just below the surface and to the rush of adrenaline, funneling it for fuel. This was a dirty little secret: there was nothing like the hunt, the throes of war, unadulterated contempt to make him feel alive.

Invigorated, he took a deep breath, straightened and strode into the adjoining room. Looking around at his men, he dared any of them to say a word about his momentary outburst.

Gazes avoided his, heads lowered, mouths twitched, but there was silence. He had worked with this group long enough for them to know better.

"John Lowry," Ryker said through clenched teeth, "is just a man. Not a legend, and soon, he'll be nothing more than collateral damage. But if anyone glorifies him again, I will cut out that man's tongue." He put his hand on the hilt of the Ka-Bar knife holstered on his hip to drive his point home.

Heads nodded.

"Sir," Two said, using judicious caution. "You didn't allow me to finish. Lowry was injured in an explosion that messed up his right leg, and he also has PTSD after being tortured and losing two men who got him out. We found meds in his cabin. Prescriptions he'll need but doesn't have. If we take precautions, he won't be a problem."

Won't be?

Did he need to buy Two a clue? John Lowry already was a problem. Zee had gotten away because of him. That was huge.

Ryker wanted Zee terrified and alone, looking over her shoulder, friendless, penniless, with no one to turn to, and when he finally had his hands wrapped around her throat, the last thing he wanted was to hear her beg for mercy that wouldn't be given. "If you're wrong and Lowry *continues* to be a problem, you'll pay for underestimating him."

A muscle ticked in Two's jaw, but he nodded.

An idea occurred to Ryker. "Tell our analyst back at headquarters to set up an alert for any prescription refills for Lowry."

"Will do." Two took out his phone and made the call.

"Prime," Seven said. "We're just now getting to her laptop. She has a ton of pictures. Taken from a live feed."

"Of what?" Ryker asked.

"Not what, sir," Seven said, shaking his head. "Who."

Ryker's pulse quickened as he hurried to the laptop that was opened in front of Seven on a desk. He pushed back the screen, leaned over and took a look.

"It's a little girl," Seven said. "I think she might have a daughter."

Ryker stared at the child. About ten years old. Long hair similar to Zee's but looser curls. Brown eyes. Skin that was closer to tan than brown. *It's her.* "Where were these pictures taken?"

"From a live feed, sir," Seven said.

A blood vessel throbbed in Ryker's temple. Was he surrounded by incompetence? "I heard you the first time. I need a location."

"I don't know, but I'm working on it. I sent the photos to our analyst and I'm going to try to extract what metadata that I can."

In the pictures, she was wearing a uniform, plaid skirt and white button-down shirt, sitting beside another child dressed the same. "It's a school," Ryker said.

But Zee wouldn't leave her with relatives, then she'd never see the child. After what happened in Germany, her father barely spoke to her. He was a cop. Her uncles were cops. She came from a long line of police officers. They would sooner turn her in than give her safe harbor or let her see her daughter as a fugitive on the run. If the girl was on her own, Zee would go for the child before disappearing again.

"A boarding school," Ryker added, "maybe one where kids can stay over Christmas break and summers. Check the west coast first, including Canada. The Midwest, too. Start with international schools that cater to kids from abroad and Christian schools. We find her," he said, pointing at the image of the child on the screen, "we'll find the target."

Knowing what alias she used to register the kid would also prove useful.

Eleven chuckled. "Then we'll have the ultimate leverage. I can't believe she was stupid enough to have a child in this business. Once we get that kid, that'll open up some interesting possibilities," he said, cracking his knuckles. "I guarantee the mom will give herself up in a heartbeat to spare her daughter any pain. She'll be such easy prey she'll come to us."

Standing upright, Ryker swung his arm, rotating his whole body to put real power behind it, and slapped the man backhanded.

Eleven staggered, his bell ringing nicely, and pressed a palm to his cheek. "What the hell?"

Ryker glared around the room at the men. "That kid…is *my* kid. If anyone lays an unauthorized hand on my daughter, I will chop it off."

"Jeez, all right," Eleven said. "We didn't know. Usually, it's no holds barred to get the target."

Ryker had a reputation that preceded him for getting the job done, whatever the job was, no matter what line had to be crossed. No matter how despicable the act. It was a reputation he enjoyed living up to.

"You neglected to brief us on this *detail*," Two said.

There hadn't been a need for them to be told. Ryker knew the child wouldn't be with her. Zee would do everything in her power not to expose their daughter to any danger, which meant keeping Olivia far away.

No one posed a bigger threat to the child than Zee did while the CIA was after her.

Ryker had claimed Olivia as his daughter in his heart a million times, but never publicly until now. Not because he hadn't wanted his little girl. *Oh*, *no*, he had wanted the child from the moment he had first tried to get Zee pregnant.

But that bitch had stripped him of paternity rights, with the Agency's help, and pretended as if he no longer existed.

He stared at the photo of Olivia. She was beautiful. Meant to be the light of his life.

Zee had stolen his kid from him. Had thrown the engagement ring in his face and refused to give them a chance to be a real family. Had deprived him of the simple joy of hearing his daughter say his name, call him *Daddy*. Had denied him the ability to be a part of Olivia's life and upbringing. Had him cast out of Langley as a respected operative, given one choice—lead cleanup teams from black sites, making the Agency's problems disappear, or lose his pension.

What kind of callous woman did that?

A heartless harpy who didn't deserve Olivia. And Zee thought he was the monster.

She had earned the hellfire that he was going to rain down upon her.

He used to keep tabs on her from afar and had abided by the CIA's leash on him, but if he had ever seen Zee with another man—someone playing daddy to Ryker's child—he would have broken the accord and broken her neck. Consequences be damned. He would've gone on the run, faced jail time, lost his daughter for good before he ever allowed Zee to replace him.

His patience and restraint were about to pay off. The tables had turned in his favor. He had no idea what her team had done wrong. All he knew was they had made a colossal mistake by becoming traitors and he was going to make the most of this golden opportunity. Show her that he indeed still existed.

Two stepped forward, looking reluctant to speak

his mind. "Does the Company know that this is personal for you, sir?"

"Of course they do," Ryker said. "Why do you think they chose me for this assignment?" No one wanted Zee dead more than he did. Smiling, he looked back at the pictures on the screen, at his daughter. His flesh and blood. He would mold her in his image and teach her to hate the woman who had kept them apart. For once, his hollow soul didn't feel empty. He was filled with righteous purpose. "This is now our top priority. We need to find my daughter and get to her first."

Chapter Seven

"Thanks again for driving us, Bill," John said.

Rubbing his wrist, he was ready to have his watch back, but his neighbor had refused to return it until their new arrangement was done.

The ride in the truck was tense and quiet. Minutes felt like hours in the strained silence. Unasked questions hung in the air: Bill's regarding Zee and what was going on, John's about why Zee needed to go to Seattle of all places, Zee's about the details surrounding his accident that had forced him out of the SEALs.

He was grateful she hadn't broached the subject. Talking about it would only dredge up ugly things he'd rather not reflect on and would only reinforce how she viewed him, as disabled.

"Sure," Bill said, casting a wary glance at Zee and the duct tape covering the bullet holes in her coat. "No problem since you're paying me."

John didn't think Bill had anything personal against her. The old guy was simply ornery with everyone. It had taken a year and a half for Bill to stop giving John a suspicious side-eye and to hold a conversation with him that lasted longer than two minutes and consisted of more words than grunts.

People out in these parts were helpful. The remote wilderness fostered a supportive community. No sticky-nosed gossip hounds getting in your business, but that also meant folks tended to look the other way during domestic disputes or when something sordid happened.

Finally, Bill pulled up to the front gate of Eielson Air Force Base and stopped the truck under the awning beside the guardhouse.

John leaned over and handed the guard his retired military ID, which was required to get them through the gate, but everyone had to show identification. Bill passed the guard his driver's license and Zee flashed her fake passport.

"All right." The guard handed everything back and waved them through.

"We're headed there," John said to Bill, pointing to the airfield. "Drop us at the passenger terminal."

Bill followed the signs, taking them to the terminal and then parking out front. "Where are you two headed?"

John smirked at the old man's curiosity getting the better of him. "The lower forty-eight," he said.

"I figured as much." Bill quirked an eyebrow. "I meant where?"

"Doesn't matter." John took the money, one thousand and two hundred dollars—a surcharge for the lift to the air force base and the logs—that he'd gotten from Zee and handed it to his neighbor. "Can I have my watch back?"

Bill touched the timepiece affectionately before unstrapping it. "This blank pan was starting to grow on me." He offered it with a frown.

Pleased to have his watch back, John glanced at the inscription.

T.O.T.S. Always.

He smiled on the inside and then he strapped it on.

John and Zee hopped out. Giving a wave of thanks to Bill, they headed into the passenger terminal.

"What does T.O.T.S. stand for?" she asked.

He shouldn't have been surprised at her perception, but she never ceased to amaze him. "Tip of the spear. The guys never wanted me to forget who I am." A special warfare operator. Now and forever.

"Why are we here?" She looked around the terminal.

There were only a handful of folks in uniform and civvies, some walking around, others seated.

"Their database is completely separate from the FAA's. That assault team," he said, lowering his voice, "or should I say the CIA, won't think to check military passenger manifests."

She didn't confirm or deny whether he was right about the CIA part. "I'd pat you on the back for this clever idea since there are no metal detectors, which also simplifies things, but they're never going to let me on a flight."

Air Mobility Command had a strict policy regarding passengers. Space available only for active duty, reservists, retirees and dependents—spouses and kids—no ordinary civilians. Even then a seat wasn't guaranteed. But if he could get them both on board this idea was a no-brainer. As long as they declared their firearms to passenger service agents, their weapons could be transported as checked luggage. And it was free. The only thing you had to pay for was an in-flight meal if you wanted one.

The trick was getting her a seat on the aircraft.

"Let me worry about that," he said, carrying her bag. "Just play along with however I decide to handle it."

"Okay."

They went up to the terminal counter.

"Good morning, sir," an affable staff sergeant said. The man had kind eyes and a genuine smile. "What can I do for you?"

After three years, it still felt odd to hear *good morning* when it was dark as night outside at ten.

"Morning," John said. "You guys have regular flights to Lewis-McChord, don't you?" It was a joint army and air force base near Tacoma, Washington, forty to fifty miles south of Seattle.

"Sure do," the sergeant said. "Several times a week. Our last flight before Christmas is actually today. Leaves in an hour."

John gave Zee an optimistic grin which was met with a skeptical frown. "Do you happen to have two seats available?" he asked.

The sergeant checked, looking down at the computer and typing on the keyboard.

John glanced around, making sure nobody else was within immediate earshot and then gave the staff sergeant a once-over, sizing him up in anticipation of the forthcoming problem. A bribe wouldn't work on this Dudley-Do-Right. Getting irate and taking the poor customer service approach only worked in the civilian world. The customer wasn't always right when it came to the military. But John noticed his wedding ring and hoped a sentimental appeal might work.

"You're in luck," the staff sergeant said. "We have plenty of room, sir. Most folks have already taken off for the holidays."

Even better. John's grin at Zee widened and her grimace deepened. She must have forgotten the part about playing along.

The staff sergeant looked up. "I just need to see some identification."

John put his ID down, took the passport from Zee and slid it across on the counter.

"Ma'am, I'm going to need to see your CAC," the sergeant said, referring to the Common Access Card issued to everyone affiliated with the military.

Zee's gaze slid to John. "She doesn't have one," he said.

The staff sergeant glanced between them. "Uh, I'm afraid I can't issue her a ticket. She's not authorized to fly with her CAC, sir."

Zee's expression turned to one that screamed *I told you so*.

John handed her the duffel. "Sweetheart, would you mind taking a seat over there." He hiked his chin at the waiting area and then leaned over to whisper in her ear. "In a minute, when the sergeant looks at you, flash him a hopeful smile." He gave her a peck on the cheek.

"Okay, *darling*. Whatever you say." She strode off to the seats.

John turned back to the airman, noting his name tag. "Staff Sergeant Torres, I need your help here."

"There's nothing I can do, sir. It's against regulations for her to fly."

"Do you remember what it was like falling in love and proposing to your wife?"

Torres sighed as his face softened. "Yeah, I do." He tried to bite back a smile and failed.

"I gave the Navy SEALs my best years. Do you know what I have to show for it besides this," he said, tapping the face of his wristwatch, "and a bum leg…?"

"No."

"Her." John hiked a thumb over his shoulder and then followed the staff sergeant's gaze.

Zee flashed a tempered smile, equal parts innocent and sexy, and his heart moved in his chest.

None of it was real, he reminded himself.

He spun back to the officer. "I want to spend the rest of my life with that woman. I blew my savings on an engagement ring." He patted the upper pocket of his coat. "And sprung for a fancy suite in Seattle. I'm planning to pop the question at the top of the Space Needle overlooking the city on Christmas Eve."

"Sounds sweet, sir. She'll brag to her friends about that forever. I wish I could've afforded something that lavish for my wife."

"That's just it—I'm so crazy in love, I wasn't thinking straight. I spent so much money on the ring and hotel I can't afford to fly us commercial.

Come on, Staff Sergeant Torres. She's going to be my wife," he said, his voice dipping softer. "Practically my dependent already. If I don't pull this off, I think she'll dump me."

Taking a deep breath, Torres lowered his gaze. He chewed on his bottom lip, debating.

"My hotel reservation was a special and it's non-refundable, man," John pleaded. "Just this once, in the spirit of Christmas, for the sake of true love, will you make an exception?"

Torres looked around. "All right. The flight is empty anyway. In the system, I'll list her as your spouse."

"Thanks, buddy."

"We don't get many SEALs through here. I'm honored to help."

"What kind of bird are we flying on?"

"C-130."

Slow and noisy, not very comfortable, but you could stretch out and sleep if there were enough empty sidewall seats. The toilets didn't offer much privacy, basically a porta potty behind a screen. But the plane was reliable, they were getting on it and that was sufficient.

It would be his first time on one since his discharge.

The airman printed up the boarding passes and handed them over. "Boarding starts in half an hour. You two made it just in time." Torres leaned forward. "Good luck with the proposal."

"You're a lifesaver. Truly." John thanked him again and crossed the space, sitting down beside Zee.

"Well?" she asked.

He handed her a boarding pass.

"How did you manage this?"

"I gave him a sob story about us being in love," John said, tension seeping through him, "and how I was going to pop the question to you at the top of the Space Needle." He pulled his gaze from her and stared at the floor. All of it was a crock. The reality wasn't the least bit rosy. "The staff sergeant bought it hook, line and sinker." Torres was as big of a sucker as John was apparently. "Nothing to it."

Zee took his face in both of her hands and then she was kissing him, and her mouth was… *God*, her mouth was sweet and too good at what it was doing—a hard, slow, thorough kiss that made his insides leap and spark to life.

Again, a sense of familiarity stole in, as if he'd known her all his life or would for the rest.

She twined her arms around his neck in a tight hug and pressed her cheek to his. Over the rush of his heartbeat thrumming in his ears, he heard her say, "I had to make it look good. He's watching us." She eased back and smiled at John, brightly, falsely.

He looked at the ticket counter.

Torres beamed and gave him a thumbs-up.

John forced a grin and a nod in return at the airman, feeling like a fool for believing, even for a split second, that the kiss and that accompanying feeling had been real.

"The lip-lock wasn't necessary," he snapped at her, holding that stupid grin on his face in case the staff sergeant was still watching. "I wish you hadn't done it."

She should *not* have kissed him because the last thing he should be thinking about after the incident in the cabin was kissing her again and that's exactly what he was doing. Thinking about pulling her into his arms and kissing her a whole hell of a lot more with no regard for onlookers.

It was only hormones, he told himself, a ridiculous spike of testosterone, a normal male reaction to a sexy woman brought on by his past three years of celibacy.

Zee gave a one-shoulder shrug. "The guy looked like he was expecting to see fireworks or something. You told me to play along."

Now she gets it.

"I'm sorry," she continued. "Obviously it was a big mistake. It didn't mean anything. The kiss was only for show."

Any more displays of inconsequential affection and he might lose his mind. "Wow. You. Are. Good. All this time, everything between us has been one big lie. You've just been acting, haven't you?" He scrubbed his palms over his thighs, his flesh beginning to itch beneath his skin.

"Our friendship is real." She put a hand on his shoulder. "It has been from the start."

He didn't want to think about the start: her knocking on his door to literally borrow a cup of sugar and offering to pay him back with a home-baked pie. He didn't want to think about all the little things in between that had saved him from his self-imposed solitude: games of chess, fishing, playing cards, fire-side chats over a glass of wine, trading chopped fire-wood for cinnamon rolls and butterscotch blondies and muffins. He definitely didn't want to think about how this was going to end.

Raking his hair back, he jumped to his feet, need-ing to move, needing to breathe. Why was it so stuffy in there? "I'm going to grab a coffee—you want something?"

She stood in front of him. "I'll go get it. You take a seat."

Rolling his eyes, he tugged at the collar of his turtleneck. "Enough coddling me—I'm capable of getting us something to drink."

"I know you are." Zee put her hand on his chest. "It's just—"

"Just what? Huh?"

"You're tired, John." She slid her hand up to his cheek. "You get cranky when you're tired."

Or when he'd been under too much stress without taking his meds.

John had considered swinging by his place on the way to Bill's to grab his medication. The odds were low that the assault team was watching his cabin, but it wasn't a chance worth taking. Missing two days' worth of doses and the lack of sleep was a bad combination.

"All right." He sat. "I'm sorry."

"Don't worry about it." She ran her hand through his hair and kissed his forehead.

All for show, of course, and if that staff sergeant's gaze hadn't been focused on them, he would've swatted her hand away and wiped the feel of her lips from his brow.

"I'll get us some food," she said. "You need to eat, get your blood sugar up." She walked away.

Restlessness coiled through him, tightening in his limbs. John got up, rolling his shoulders, and strolled to the wall of windows overlooking the aircraft on the apron.

This was how the crippling anxiety started without his meds. Restlessness that swelled into unease that had the potential to cascade into full-blown agitation. Drop him in the middle of a city, lots of people, heavy traffic, a sensory overload of sounds, the crush of pedestrians on the sidewalks…and then the static in his head would kick in—a roar of white noise.

More flashbacks and dissociation were a possibility, too.

Prevention was key, knowing his triggers. Stress. Fatigue. Cities. Explosions. Fights. Large groups of people. Being around his old teammates.

He could prevent one out of seven. Not too bad. He rubbed a hand across the scruff on his jaw, thinking of ways to mitigate his symptoms before they worsened.

Sleep always helped. If he slept on the flight, he might be able to function. Muster through to get Zee someplace safe.

He didn't want to unravel in public. Not in front of her. At times, he hated being this changed man, different than who he'd been for almost two decades. As a SEAL sleep deprivation had often come with the territory, in BUD/S—Basic Underwater Demolition/ SEAL—training, out on long missions. Always, he'd coped, had managed to push through. Now fatigue wasn't something he could overcome and conquer.

If he weren't careful, it would conquer him.

Pressing a palm to his forehead, he stared out the window at the C-130 Hercules sitting under the bright lights of the apron. That plane was probably going to be their ride. Off to the side, not too far away, was a helicopter.

Big. Black. The same freaking model as the assault helicopter from last night.

Icy calm stole over him, his heartbeat slowing down. He needed all his senses and wits about him if that strike team was here on Eielson with them.

His gaze flickered up at the movement in the reflection of the window.

One of the Delta operators walked through the terminal. He was wearing all-black utility gear, tactical boots, a sidearm hooked on his hip.

The man strode up to Torres. "When will the helicopter be finished refueling?"

Thankfully he didn't keep his voice down.

"One more aircraft, then yours. About two more hours. Did you need it sooner?"

The guy from the strike team shrugged. "We don't have a destination yet. I needed an update, but would you mind bumping us up? Just in case. If we get a bead on a location, we'll need to move fast, and I don't want it to be my fault if that bird isn't fueled and ready to go."

While the two men continued to chat, John lowered his head, scratching his brow to hide his profile, and beat a path in the direction Zee had gone. He chose to leave the duffel bag behind on a chair. No one would touch it during the few minutes he'd be gone and going back to the seats for the bag might draw unwanted attention.

The pressing matter was that Zee might pop up at any minute, completely unaware that danger had waltzed in, and he didn't want that operator spotting her. Then all hell would break loose and their exit out of Alaska would be a bust.

Picking up his pace slightly—he didn't want to appear to be in a rush—he headed for the lone coffee shop. She was at the far end of the counter, waiting for an order that was probably for him. She loved her coffee black with no sugar, and he tolerated the same, but he loved a good cappuccino. Whenever she went into town for him, she'd always pick one up.

The barista handed Zee two cups with lids and a bag as he entered. "Black coffee, decaf cappuccino, and I heated those sandwiches for you."

Decaf?

She caught the look on his face. "What's wrong?"

"They're here on base. One from Delta is at the ticket counter."

"Damn it," she said, her voice thin with shock, almost so soundless that she had practically mouthed the words.

"He didn't see me." Sheer dumb luck that the guy from Delta hadn't spotted her either on his way in. The man had passed right by the coffee shop.

John ushered her to the back corner of the café

where there was a bathroom. He checked the door. It was unoccupied and they ducked inside. Maintaining a crack in the door, he kept an eye on the main corridor so he could see when the operative left.

"He was asking about the refuel time on their helicopter," John said.

"It should've occurred to me that they might come here. Sometimes the Agency will use bases as way stations for lodging and fuel, especially in remote locations such as this. Clearance goes through in a snap. No one asks questions and everyone will stay out of their way."

He glanced at her. "So this is the CIA?" When she hesitated, he said, "I'm in this. For better or worse." Immediately he regretted the poor choice of words. "You know what I mean. I think we've established I have a need to know and I can be trusted."

"Yes, it's the CIA."

He shifted his gaze back to the corridor.

"It was never about not trusting you," she said. "The less you know, the better. To keep you safe."

"Yeah, yeah." The operative strolled past and out the front doors, none the wiser. "It's clear. He's gone."

"Did he say where they're headed?" she asked.

He shook his head. "No, he had no idea. They don't have a location yet, which means they don't know where you are or where you're going."

Relief shone in her gaze and she sagged against the wall. "Good. Let's hope they keep spinning their wheels. What do we do in the meantime?"

"Thirty minutes until we board. I think it's safe

for us to wait in the terminal. Doubtful they'll be back before we leave, but I suggest putting your hair up as a precaution." She had striking curls that were distinctive and noticeable. "And I'll scrounge up a ball cap for myself."

She set the things in her hands down on the bathroom counter. Looking in the mirror, she gathered her lush curls into a bundle and twisted the hair into a topknot that held its form without the help of pins or an elastic band.

"You need to eat." She handed him one of the cups and the bag as they left the bathroom.

His stomach rumbled with hunger. Starving, he peeked in the bag. It smelled good. The sandwich would be perfect. A decent helping of healthy carbs and protein would make him feel better.

Looking him over, she pressed a palm to his forehead.

He swatted away her warm hand that time. "Stop it." At the sharpness in his voice, he realized he was beginning to prickle in defensiveness and needed to take it down a notch.

"Are you going to be okay?"

"Sure." The response was automatic. After it came out of his mouth, he took stock of his condition. The truth was he was embarrassed by the timing of this, that *this* was an issue for him at all. He should tell her, wanted to explain what was happening to him, but it felt like weakness. Deep down he knew it was biochemical. Something had gotten scrambled in his brain after he'd been tortured and with the explosion during the escape that had killed two of his guys and messed up his leg. Still, it felt like weakness. "I can't believe you got me decaf," he said, wanting to change the subject.

"You need sleep on the flight." She circled right back to the topic he sought to avoid. "You're on edge, wound up too tight."

She had no idea, and he prayed that his condition wouldn't worsen to the point that she found out. But he feared that he wouldn't get better unless he got his medication.

"It'll pass," he said. "I'll be fine once I eat and get some rest."

Watching him intently, she nodded, but doubt gleamed in her eyes. "I hope so."

Chapter Eight

By the time they reached the passenger terminal at Joint Base Lewis-McChord, John wasn't looking any better and was far from being himself. He was ghostly pale, not just ashen, but a sickly pallor. Of greater concern to Zee was that he wouldn't make eye contact with her.

During the five-hour flight, he had stretched out across almost four seats and tried to rest. But it wasn't the deep REM sleep that he needed. Maybe it had been the adrenaline, maybe it had been the deafening roar of the engine, or the uncomfortable seats that had kept him tossing every five minutes.

Whatever the issue, Zee was worried about him. "You got me out of Alaska and to Tacoma. This is above and beyond," she said. "Whatever vow you made to me I release you from it."

John took off his ball cap and wiped his sweat-covered brow with the back of his hand. "This isn't Seattle and you're still not safe." He hoisted her duffel bag on his shoulder and walked away from her going to the ticket counter.

Arguing with him was pointless. She was learning that the hard way. Once John had set his mind to something, he saw it through to the end.

She only wanted to keep everyone she cared about safe.

At the terminal counter, John made arrangements for a ride with the airman on duty.

The airman ordered a Lyft, using base mode in the app. It ensured the driver who was matched would have access to get through the front gate because they already had a CAC. As their destination, she gave the address of a coffee shop one block from her true objective, and she used her prepaid VISA card to cover the fare.

They waited for their driver, Peter, in the vestibule. Estimated time of arrival was twenty-two minutes.

Once the car arrived, they climbed into the sedan. It was an older Hyundai. Silver. She saw it had over 130,000 miles.

"Hey, Peter, we need to go to more than one destination," she said, thinking long-term.

His brows drew together. "Only one location was entered and paid for on the app."

"Yep, and I'm willing to pay you five thousand more, in cash, to give us your car."

Both John and Peter stared at her.

"I need this car to get to the base for my day job and for my side hustle at night." The kid was about twenty years old.

She unzipped her bag and pulled out the cash. "I'm guessing this beater is worth two grand. Four tops." She offered the money. "That means you make a profit." The car wouldn't stand out, would blend in, and if he was using it to cart people around, she figured it was well maintained and reliable, too.

"Are you for real?" Peter asked.

"Yes. I am."

Peter clenched the steering wheel. "I don't know."

John hit the button on the door with a trembling hand, sending the window buzzing down. He stuck his head outside and took deep breaths.

What was wrong with him? Was he coming down with something?

Zee pulled out an extra bundle of cash. "Ten grand. You can buy another car, take a vacation and have money in your pocket for a nice holiday season."

"I think she wants you to retire," John said.

At least he hadn't lost his sense of humor. She'd take what she could get. "My final offer, Peter. Take it or I'll find someone else who will."

"Yeah, yeah, all right." Peter snatched the money. "I'll take it."

"Do you need us to drop you someplace close by?" she offered.

"Nah, I live on base in the barracks." He jumped out, keeping the driver's door open, and thumbed through the money.

Zee left John in the back along with the duffel bag and slipped in behind the wheel.

"Have a merry Christmas and a happy New Year!" Peter waved as Zee pulled off.

John tipped his head back on the seat with the window down, letting in the frigid air. He wasn't okay, so she wasn't going to ask a question that had an obvious answer.

"Did you sleep at all on the flight?" she asked.

"No. The engine was too loud. The noise was a trigger that made it worse."

"Made what worse?"

Shutting his eyes, he pinched the bridge of his nose. "Nothing."

He wanted her to trust him with her secrets and rely on him for support, but he wasn't willing to do the same in return.

This wasn't going to work.

"What do you need, John?" Food hadn't helped, and he definitely needed something. "What can I get you?"

"I'm fine."

But he wasn't. She only wanted to help him, to protect him, and he wouldn't let her.

The one-hour ride was awkward with both of them keeping secrets. He probably thought his reason was as justified as hers. She knew how dangerous secrets could be.

Her ex had lied to her from day one about everything. Had used manipulation and coercion to keep her close. She vowed never to go through that again.

There were similarities between Ryker and John. Two sides of the same coin. She'd be a blind fool not to acknowledge it, but the fundamental differences between them far outweighed anything they had in common.

Whatever John was hiding, she sensed it was related to his military service and to the reason he was no longer in the navy. That was the one touchy subject for him that he had difficulty sharing.

If they were going to stick this out together, then she'd push for them both to put all their cards on the table. But that wasn't part of her plan.

Nothing had changed. The only way for John to be safe was if he were far away from her. And she was set on making that a reality.

She parked the car at the front entrance of the sprawling campus of the all-girls Emerald City Academy for grades three through twelve.

John lifted his head from the backseat like he had a sixth sense that they'd reached their destination and opened his eyes. "What are we doing here?" Sitting up, he looked around. "Is this a school?"

"Wait here." She turned off the ignition and pocketed the keys. "Better yet, take what cash you need from the bag and lie low in a hotel for a week or so. Okay?" If she trusted him with her life, she could trust him with her money. "You've done more than enough to help me. I'm grateful. *Please* believe me."

One day, she'd send him a letter expressing not only the depths of her gratitude but also her true feelings for him. For now, he needed to go.

He leaned forward, putting a hand on the back of her seat. "Zee, think of me as a boomerang. You can throw me away, really put your arm into it if it makes you feel any better, but I'll just come right back. Until you're safe." His gaze bounced around, avoiding hers, and flicked up to the rearview mirror. "And that's not here in the middle of Seattle with only God knows how many CCTV cameras for Delta to tap into and locate you via face recognition."

It wasn't lost on her that when thrown properly, boomerangs were lethal weapons. "By the time they get here, I'll be long gone."

"They're already here."

She stiffened. "What are you talking about?"

"In the rearview mirror, I spotted three black SUVs, large enough to hold a baker's dozen of those Delta boys, headed toward the west side of the school. Could be coincidence, but my gut is telling me that it's not."

That meant Delta team had recovered her laptop and were probably in the process of doing a deep dive into her hard drive, extracting any data that might be useful.

She shoved the thought aside. For now, thinking about the hard drive was a distraction. She had a far more pressing problem.

On the west end of the school was the seldom-used entrance for VIPs. It was probably the easiest access point for them to breach discreetly.

How had she missed their arrival?

She glanced in the rearview mirror, but of course there was nothing to see. The one bright spot in this was that regardless of what was going on with John, he was cognizant and competent, and she hoped still physically capable.

"Why are we here?" he asked.

"I'm not answering that question and I'm not letting you go inside that school with me unless you tell me what's wrong with you. Tick, tock, John." She was moving out in five seconds, with or without him.

"I don't have my meds." He squeezed his eyes shut. "For my PTSD." The agony in his voice sounded like it was choking him.

It was all she could do not to hold him close and hug until her arms ached, then find a way to get him his medication. But there was no time. She had to move. "Can you handle going in there?"

His eyes flew open. "Yes," he said without a second of hesitation, his gaze holding hers *finally*.

"Come on."

They alighted from the car and made a beeline for the entrance.

"What do you take?" she asked.

"Sertraline, fifty milligrams twice a day. Most days anyway."

The front doors were locked per protocol. She waved at the camera so someone inside would buzz them in.

"How many doses have you missed?" she asked.

"I'm going on five. If I were in the woods, with peace and quiet, sticking to my routine, it wouldn't be a problem. That's how I can go a few days at a time without it."

Oh, John. He was in pain and it was her fault. His suffering made her heart hurt.

She wanted him to go back to the car, wait for her there, but he'd only take offense, and she'd done too much damage already. "You should've told me. I would've understood."

It bothered her, deep down in a way she barely

comprehended, that he hadn't trusted her enough to confide something so important. She'd thought them closer than this. The only secrets she'd kept from John were those to protect him or Olivia. This was different.

The buzzer rang, the lock disengaged and she opened the door.

"Are you going to make me ask you again?" he pressed, his tone implying he wouldn't drop it until he got an answer.

Since he had shared, something that seemed difficult for him to admit, it was time for her to do likewise. "We're here to get my daughter," she said, walking into the building.

John stumbled across the threshold behind her, and she realized it wasn't because of his leg injury. Any shock he was feeling was to be expected.

"Are you angry with me?" she wondered. "For not telling you about her. I thought it was the best way to keep her safe." It was never to be dishonest with John or hide the fact that she had a daughter. Her number-one role in life, the thing she was most proud of was being a mother.

John shook his head. "Ditto."

"What does that mean?"

"You should've told me. I would've understood."

And in that moment, she fell a little harder for John. "Olivia means everything to me. There's nothing in this world that's more important to me than her."

"We'll get her." He put a hand on her shoulder. "I might look like I'm in rough shape, but I won't let you down." His voice was ironclad with determination.

Nodding, she had every confidence that John would follow through on his pledge.

In the front office, she signed in at the desk. "Hi, I'm Zoey Howard, here to pick up my daughter, Olivia, for the holiday break."

"Certainly." An elderly woman got up from a desk that was situated farther back in the room and came to the front. "May I see some—"

Zee showed her one of her fake IDs.

"Oh, you're prepared for the drill." The older woman, a short plump gray-haired lady, put on her glasses and took a look. "What class is she assigned to?"

"She is in the sixth grade, Ms. Colvin's homeroom."

Her daughter was a Christmas baby and would turn eleven in two days. To bypass the rule in Virginia that children had to be five before September 30 to be eligible for kindergarten, Zee had put Olivia in private school. When they went on the run, her little girl had to take an entrance exam for the Emerald City Academy. Olivia had scored remarkably high. Turned out that her daughter was gifted and was able to skip the fifth grade.

The principal of the academy had worried that putting Olivia in the sixth grade at such a young age might negatively impact her social and emotional development, but Zee saw it as an extra layer of protection.

Anyone trying to find her daughter would be

looking for a little girl in the fifth grade. Not the sixth.

The woman looked Olivia up in the computer. "It says here that you weren't going to pick her up for the winter break."

"Change of plans." She'd wanted nothing more than to spend the one day a year with her daughter that they had dubbed a double holiday, Olivia's birthday and Christmas rolled into one—*Olivmas*. The one day the CIA would triple their efforts looking for her because emotion might lure her out of hiding and to her daughter. Zee had worried about getting spotted on CCTV in an airport, hotel, on the streets of Seattle, and exposing her daughter to unnecessary danger. But look at them now. Danger was breaking in through the west gate. "I was able to take time off from work and so was my fiancé." She gestured to John.

He smiled and nodded, looking like he might pass out at any minute.

"Okay," the woman said, not seeming to notice John's sickly appearance. "I made a note in the system. I'll call for her." She reached for the public address system that they used to announce a parent's arrival and to send for the children.

This was the preferred method Zee had used two previous times. It limited her exposure on the school's security feeds and she didn't have to interact with anyone else inside the building. But advertising her arrival and broadcasting that Olivia could be intercepted on her way to the front office was the last thing she needed.

"No." Zee's sharp tone elicited a raised brow from the woman. "I want to surprise her. We'll go get her. And one more thing. I saw some suspicious men lurking on the west side of the school," Zee said. "They looked like they were up to no good. I'd feel a heck of a lot better as I'm sure every parent of a child here would, if you called the police. Right away. Tell them it's an emergency."

"I could've sworn at least one had a gun," John said. "I'd hate to think that they were here to kidnap a child."

Alarm streaked across the woman's face. "Oh, dear."

Zee began ushering John out the office door and into the corridor of the school.

The woman picked up the phone. "Thank you for telling me. I will also get our security team on it."

Police would have a difficult time facing off against Delta. School security guards wouldn't stand a chance.

Getting Olivia out of there as quickly as possible might be the only way to save innocent lives.

As the guard's radio squawked, Ryker squeezed the trigger, putting a bullet in his forehead. The man was dead before he crumpled to the ground.

"According to the online schedule," Two said, "the fifth graders have dinner at this time."

"Everyone, move out to the cafeteria," Ryker said. "Except for Two, Eleven and Five. Find her room and check there as a precaution." Not everyone ate at the same pace and some probably preferred to eat in their rooms. He wanted all bases covered in any eventuality. "Pack a bag with some of her stuff, too. Essentials." He didn't want the hassle of the kid needing something while he was still focused on finding and terminating Zee. "No one is to hurt my kid. And try not to kill any others." That last part seemed like something a father should say, but Ryker didn't feel any repugnance over some other child getting caught in the crossfire. He felt absolutely nothing besides the desire to claim his daughter like a conqueror and lay waste to Zenobia, leaving her as nothing more than scorched earth.

His men nodded and dispersed, following the order.

Ryker led the main team to the cafeteria. They crossed the spacious open-air courtyard, a quadrangle that the school was built around. He imagined Olivia sitting outside on a bench in pleasant weather, reading a book, giggling with her friends, kicking around a ball. This was a posh school. Expensive. A beautiful place for people to dump their offspring. Must have taken all of Zee's savings. Probably offered one of the best educations.

Once Zee was dead, he'd put his daughter in one similar on the East Coast. All girls, too, with no boys as a distraction. Someplace safe where Olivia would be watched over while he was away on assignments, taking lives and crossing out names on the CIA's hit list.

Their time together might be limited, but he would ensure it'd be precious, cherished. Fun. Enough to train her, shape her and teach her to be loyal to him above all else.

He would sow the necessary seeds and reap her unconditional love.

That was how he'd give Olivia Jekyll, so that she never saw Hyde.

ZEE HAD MILES of hallway to navigate before they made it to the third floor of the dormitory that housed the fifth and sixth graders. Zee raced down the corridor with John at her side, their footfalls not making a sound. Unlike the rest of the school, the halls in the dorm were carpeted.

Olivia kept to a strict schedule that Zee had memorized. Her daughter always read in her room before dinner for at least thirty minutes.

Kids were assigned rooms based on their grade and last name. She glanced at the name tags along the way, stopping at the one at the end of the hall that read: Hoffman, Madison. Howard, Olivia.

She knocked then twisted the knob and flung open the door.

A startled brunette with braided pigtails, sitting cross-legged on top of her bed, looked up from a book she was reading. It was Olivia's best friend, Madison.

Zee's gaze swept across the large room, to the second empty bed and over to the sitting area with two desks.

Where was Olivia?

Zee looked back at the girl. "Hi, Madison." She stepped inside and John followed her, sticking close to her heels. "I'm Olivia's mom. Where is she?" Zee hoped for a bit a luck that her daughter was only down the hall in the bathroom.

"Hi, Mrs. Howard." Madison set her book to the side. Pushing her glasses up the bridge of her nose, she climbed down from the bed and proffered her hand. "It's so nice to finally meet you. She talks about you all the time," Madison said, shaking Zee's hand. "It was great of you to give her permission to come home with me for Hanukkah since my parents were back in the country. We had so much fun together. It was awesome to have a friend to hang out with at home for once."

"She told me how much she enjoyed it, too." Zee tamped back her rising panic over her daughter's whereabouts. "It was nice of you to invite her." A kindness that Zee had appreciated, unable to spend quality time with her daughter herself. Zee was aware that the friendship had become a lifeline for both girls. "Madison, we're in a bit of a rush. Where's Olivia? I really need to get her so we can go," she said, grabbing her daughter's coat from a hook.

"You're taking her?" Disappointment and surprise washed over Madison's face. "We thought we'd be together for the winter break. We had the whole thing planned." Her shoulders slumped. "Now I've got to spend it alone?"

Ripping Olivia away from the sanctuary of EC Academy and destroying the little sense of normalcy that she'd found wasn't what Zee wanted. Her daughter didn't deserve this upheaval in her young life. But it was unavoidable.

"Madison," Zee said, pointedly, while trying to keep her anxiety out of her tone. She didn't want to scare her. "Where is Olivia? It's important I find her right now."

The little girl sighed. "She was hungry and decided to go to the cafeteria early for dinner with the elementary kids."

The response sent fear spiraling through Zee as her stomach went hollow.

CLEARLY MARKED SIGNS guided Ryker and his team down the halls and around the bends. The temperature in the building was perfect like everything else one would expect from a place like this. Not too hot, not too cool. Even the air was faintly scented with lemon.

He took out one more guard along the way, a double tap to the chest. By the time his team was finished, there would be quite a mess of bodies to clean up.

They pushed open the double doors to the cafeteria and swept inside. The girls were all chatting and eating in clusters like normal kids would, not paying attention to anything around them.

Then one child noticed Ryker and his team, followed by another and another. A hush fell over the dining hall as gazes swung their way. The screams came next, like fingernails on a chalkboard.

"We're not here to hurt anyone!" Ryker said, lowering his gun. He waved at his men to also lower their weapons. The sooner he got the frenzy under control the easier this would be.

The kids in the cafeteria ranged from eight years old to ten, possibly eleven. There weren't many of them. Maybe seventy at most. But after a cursory glance, he didn't spot Olivia.

"Point out the fifth graders and we'll leave," Ryker said. His thinking was that birds of a feather flocked together. Or rather those in the same grade would congregate.

One lone finger pointed to tables at the far side of the cafeteria, and others were quick to confirm where he'd find his daughter.

He strode to the other side of the dining hall as the girls cowered, keeping their heads bent. Walking in between tables, he looked them over, one by one.

There!

At the last table, he spotted a girl with long dark hair, her head hung with her chin to her chest. Her spiral curls shrouded her face like a curtain.

A euphoric jolt of victory zinged through him. "Olivia!" He ran over to her, put his hand on her shoulder and spun her around.

The terrified face that looked up at him wasn't his daughter's.

Chapter Nine

At the sound of footsteps in the hall, Zee whirled around as a shadow fell over the doorway. Her heart leaped into her throat. Men had silently crept up on them as a result of the carpet.

John lunged across the threshold shoving them back.

"Get down!" Zee instructed the little girl, and Madison dove for the floor.

A third man fired into the room, narrowly missing Zee and shooting a desk. Dropping her daughter's things, she snatched her baton from the holster and extended it with the flick of her wrist.

She threw a boot heel into the man's gut, kicking him into the hall to avoid Madison getting hit by any stray shots. Whipping the baton up, she struck the man's firing arm, sending it into the air and knocking the gun loose from his grip. Then she went for his head and kept swinging until he dropped and stopped moving.

John had disarmed two men, shot one and cold-cocked the other. Sweat beaded on his face like he had just sprinted a four-minute mile and rolled down his temples as a tremor ran through him. But he was steady on his feet and his reflexes were sharp.

Zee knelt beside the man she'd bludgeoned into unconsciousness and grabbed his earpiece. Putting on the Bluetooth comms device, she needed to stay abreast of Delta team's movements in the school and whether or not they'd found Olivia.

No way in hell they were leaving the premises with her daughter. She'd tear them all to pieces first.

Standing, she spun toward movement in the hallway.

Olivia. Her daughter stood five doors down, wide-eyed and frozen, holding a to-go container.

Zee dashed down the hall, whisked her daughter into her arms and hugged her close to her chest. *Thank God.* Olivia was safe and in her embrace.

"Mom?" Olivia's arms wrapped around her neck. "What are you doing here? What's going on?"

"I'll explain later. We have to go." Hugging her little girl tighter, her heart overflowing with relief, Zee stroked Olivia's hair that was up in a ponytail and kissed the top of her head.

Never wanting to let her go, Zee forced herself to break the embrace. She held her daughter at arm's length and looked her over from head to toe.

"Go?" Olivia asked. "Where?"

"Mockingjay," Zee said, using the code to tell her daughter everything she needed to know in the moment with a single word: they had to run, time was pressing, their lives were in danger. Olivia loved *The Hunger Games* series of books and Zee knew that she'd never forget what it meant. Other than keeping her daughter safe, preparing her for whatever might come was the next best thing she could do.

Olivia went rigid and pulled away from her. All questions and confusion drained from her expression. "I have to get my go bag." She turned and rushed down the hall to her room.

Zee was right behind her, worried that goodbyes with Madison would slow them down.

Olivia grabbed her coat from the floor, throwing it on as she passed Madison, who stood in the middle of the room, agape, her face pale and stark with horror. Olivia snatched a backpack from her closet and shoved the wrapped Olivmas present that Zee had sent her inside the bag.

Her daughter hurried up to her roommate and threw her arms around her in a hug. "I'll miss you, Madison. You're the best friend I've ever had." Then Olivia let her go and walked out of the room without a glance back.

Zee was proud that her daughter was so strong and brave, but it saddened her even more that Olivia had to be this tough at such a young age. It wasn't right.

She took her daughter's free hand since she was still holding the to-go container and the three of them ran to the stairwell.

"This is Prime," a familiar voice said in Zee's ear over Delta's comms, and she tripped down two steps as her heart seized. No, it couldn't be him. *Dear God, please, not him.* "My daughter isn't in the cafeteria. Delta Two, you better have her. Report."

Blistering shock seared through her. Hot nausea boiled in her throat.

No, no, no. "Ryker," she muttered to herself.

"WHO'S RYKER?" JOHN ASKED, wondering why they had stopped moving. Static hadn't started blaring in his head, yet, but once the white noise kicked in, he didn't know how much good he'd be and would prefer to make tracks before that happened.

Zee stood frozen, looking shaken as if she'd seen a ghost. "We have to get out of here."

His sentiments exactly.

They hustled down to the main floor and ran along the corridor, leaving the dormitory section. Scrambling around the bend, they hurried down the hall toward the entrance and passed a wall of windows that overlooked the open-air quad at the heart of the school.

Zee's attention whipped outside as she slowed.

John followed her line of sight. Across the way, on the other side of the courtyard in the parallel section of the school, was Delta team.

One man caught sight of them as well and slowed to a stop. Mr. Trench Coat.

There wasn't a door leading to the quad in the hallway they were in. The rest of Delta took off down the corridor, no doubt headed their way.

But Trench Coat just stood there for a second, the same way he had at the lake. Back then, John had thought the man was being cavalier about the situation. Now he suspected it was something else entirely and far worse.

Trench Coat raised his weapon and opened fire, shooting out the windows in his own hallway. He leaped over the sill past the shards jutting around the frame. Firing more rounds, he bounded across the courtyard.

Zee lowered Olivia's head, shielding her as she also ducked. The windows in their corridor shattered under the continued gunfire. Bullets hammered into the inside wall opposite of where they were positioned as Olivia gave a startled cry.

John threw his arms around both of them and made a beeline for the entrance.

"Zenobia!" a man called out, and John guessed it was Trench Coat. "Zee!" Her name echoed with rage in the corridor. "Give her to me and I'll kill you quickly!"

Police rushed inside the building and down the hall from the entrance, weapons drawn.

The woman from the front desk was behind the four officers and beckoned to them. "Mrs. Howard, come this way."

"Those crazy men are shooting," Zee said, pointing back behind her. "You have to hurry."

John stole a glance over his shoulder as Delta team rounded the corner, joining up with Trench Coat who had just jumped into the corridor.

"Freeze!" one cop said. "Drop your weapons and put—"

The *pip pip* of suppressed gunfire whispered in the air. A series of rapid bangs rang out as the officers returned fire.

"Zenobia!" Trench Coat said.

The older gray-haired woman yelped and scurried into the main office.

John put Zee and Olivia in front of him, using

his body to shield them from the incoming barrage. They bulled through the doors into the vestibule and shoved through the next set outside.

Hustling down the steps, he checked their surroundings. Two squad cars with flashing lights were parked out front. Sirens sounded in the distance drawing closer.

There was no sign of Delta team. It looked all clear, but that wouldn't last for too long. The cops would slow Delta down, not stop them.

They ran to the beater Hyundai and hopped in.

Zee peeled off, tires screeching, and whipped into traffic, cutting off another car that blared its horn. The strident sound slashed through John's head, and he rubbed at his temples.

"Stay down low," she said to her daughter.

The girl slid down in the backseat, without any questions asked and not a single whimper, as though this were routine.

Taking sharp turns and blowing the speed limit as much as traffic allowed, Zee drove like she knew where she was going.

"Where are we headed?" he asked. The tremble in his hand had gotten so bad that he crossed his arms to keep her from seeing it.

"A motel. In Issaquah. There's limited CCTV in the area. I know what exit to take so they won't be able to track us. We stayed there when I was first getting Olivia settled into the school."

He cracked the window, letting in fresh air, but didn't roll it all the way down because he didn't want the kid to catch a chill in the back.

After he checked the mirrors and was certain that they weren't being followed, he closed his eyes. Focused on taking steady deep breaths.

In the airport at Eielson, he'd been on edge, the first prickle of anxiety starting to get to him, but the plane ride, with the roar of the C-130 engine, brought everything back to him in a rush. Kept the most horrific parts of what he'd been through playing on a loop inside his head.

How he was able to function without having a complete meltdown was any wonder. Back at the school when he had taken down two operatives, instinct, training and efficiency gained from many years of practice had coalesced into action for him.

But the pressure was mounting. In his head. In his chest.

John breathed in slowly through his nose, feeling his stomach expand as he inhaled. Concentrated on filling up his lungs with air. Released the breath through his mouth. Opening his eyes, he looked around and went through the rest of the grounding technique that helped him stave off flashbacks and dissociation.

One, I see the glove box. Two, I see the freeway. Three, I see a minivan. Four, I see Christmas lights. Five, I see Zee.

So beautiful.

Closing his eyes, he strained to go through the next part.

One, I hear the hiss of the car's tires on the wet asphalt. Two, I hear the wind rushing in through the window. Three, I hear "Santa Claus Is Coming to

Town" playing on the radio. Four, I hear the crinkle of polystyrene foam. Five, I hear Zee drumming her fingers on the steering wheel.

It all came back to Zee. Goddess with a baton.

At the motel, she parked away from the check-in office and kept the engine running, the radio on. "I'll be right back." She pulled on a wool hat, covering her hair, and yanked her hood up over her head.

The door slammed and she was gone. He glanced around the dark motel parking lot. It wasn't the best neighborhood he'd been in, but it wasn't the worst either. About half the rooms appeared occupied.

In the backseat, Olivia was quiet, still slouched down, her fingers digging into the to-go container, causing it to squeak every now and again. The sound grated on his ears, making his nerves flare and his limbs twitch. But he could only imagine the riot of emotions going through the girl. For someone so young, she displayed impressive cool under pressure. Olivia had a backbone of steel, just like her mom.

Gritting his teeth, he clenched his fingers and decided to run through another grounding technique.

Two minutes later, Zee hopped back in. She pulled off and drove to a part of the lot that offered three different exits and parked in front of a room. "Let's go."

The three of them got out, with John grabbing the duffel bag from the back and hitching it onto his shoulder.

Zee unlocked the door. Flipping on the lights, she ushered them into suite that had a semiprivate bedroom and small separate sitting area. He presumed the sofa pulled out into an extra bed.

After locking the door, Zee took him by the arm over to a corner. "I have to run an errand. It'll take me an hour. Two at most."

"What's the errand? I'll go."

"No, you need to rest. Will you be okay here, alone with her?"

He wasn't quite sure what she was asking. "With my PTSD attacks I don't get violent or destructive if that's what you're worried about," he said, sounding somewhat more insulted than he wanted to let on.

Some guys from the cognitive therapy group he'd gone through at Veterans Affairs had vicious episodes on occasion, making them a danger to themselves and those around them. John prided himself on not having that type of issue.

"I trust you with my daughter," she said with unwavering confidence. "I know she'll be safe with you. I asked if you'd be okay with her. You've been under a lot of stress."

Understanding what she meant, he exhaled with relief. "I'll be fine." More like he'd hold it together for as long as necessary. "What if you get into trouble out there?" He wouldn't be able to help her.

Zee's gaze bounced to her daughter and then back to him. "I doubt that I will. On the off chance that I do, there's a letter in Olivia's go bag. My parents' address is on the envelope. Take her there."

Surprise rocked through him. She really had planned for the worst. "What about you?"

"Nothing is going to happen. I'll be back." She

pressed a palm to his chest. "Two hours tops." She crossed the room and went to Olivia. The girl had taken a seat on the sofa and looked as if she was awaiting instructions. "Honey, I have to go out, just for a little bit. My friend John is going to stay with you. He'll make sure nothing happens to you while I'm gone. When I get back, we'll talk."

She kissed her daughter's forehead, gave John one last, long look and slipped out of the room.

John put the chain on, not that it would stop someone from getting in. He sat on the floor, with his back to a dresser and his legs blocking the door as an added precaution. If he suffered a flashback or entered a dissociative trance, he didn't want to chance one of those Delta boys busting in without him being aware.

As difficult as the past twenty-four hours had been for him, it had given him a renewed sense of purpose. Serving his country had been the only career he'd ever considered. Joining Special Forces had been a calling. He'd thought for sure that he'd be a lifer.

Then he'd been captured, tortured, permanently injured, changing his destiny.

But it had also led him to Zee. To saving this little girl. He couldn't dismiss how once again he felt *called* to serve.

Taking off his coat, he kept it within easy reach. The gun he'd taken from one of the men was concealed in the pocket.

"Are you all right?" Olivia asked.

"Yeah, kiddo. I'll be fine. I'm only tired."

"You look sick."

That, too. "I'm tired and a bit under the weather, but it's nothing to concern you."

"You need chicken soup. It'll make you feel better." She took off her jacket and set her backpack down. "Is it okay if I turn on the TV?"

"Sure. My head hurts, so if you could watch a show that's not too noisy, I'd appreciate it."

She switched on the television and scrolled through the channels. Once she'd picked something, he heard her moving around the room. Then she came over, sat next to him and handed him a bottle of water.

"I put on a nature show. It's about the migration of birds. I turned the TV in case you wanted to watch it with me."

A swarm of swallows dipped across the blue sky on the television screen. "Thanks," he said, for the water and the overall consideration.

She opened her to-go container. "Do you want some?" She held the box out to him. Roasted chicken, mashed potatoes and green beans were inside.

Suddenly, he was famished. "I'm good." His stomach rumbled, betraying him.

"Are you sure? I can hear your stomach growling." Her voice was soft as cotton. "I have enough to share."

As she offered the food to him once more, he met her gaze. She resembled her mother. Same almond-shaped brown eyes. Her hair was a little longer and the mass of brown curls had natural blond highlights. The genuine smile she gave him was tentative.

It reminded him of the first time he'd met Zee. Same smile. Kind mixed with a bit of apprehension.

"You eat up." He opened the bottle of water and chugged the whole thing, hoping it would quiet his rumbling belly.

She dug into her food, and his shoulders relaxed.

"Can we play twenty questions?" she asked.

His head was killing him, and he'd rather sit quietly, but he said, "Sure. If you want."

"How do you know my mom?"

"Uh, we were neighbors."

"Where did she live?"

"I don't think this is how the game goes."

Her smile this time was less wary. "It is the way I play it." She was clever, too, like her mom.

"Alaska," he said, realizing there were probably lots of things she was curious to know. But he was surprised this was what she'd asked. "About an hour outside of Fairbanks."

"That's north of Anchorage, right?"

"Yep."

"Describe it to me. What it looked like. What the air smelled like. The air smells different here than it did in Virginia."

Somehow, this little girl got him talking. The conversation eased the tension bubbling in the back of his brain, helping him to focus intently and stay grounded. All good things.

Before he knew it, a key was shoved in the lock and the door opened, catching on the chain. "John," Zee said.

"Right here." He climbed to his feet and let her in.

Zee walked through the room carrying shopping bags. After setting everything down, she roped

Olivia into a big hug and kissed her cheeks and fore-head like she couldn't get enough of her. "Hungry?"

"No, I ate the food from the school."

Zee fished out pajamas from the bag and gave them to her daughter. "Go run a bath," she said, opening a container and then dumped two gummy pills into Olivia's palm. "I'll be there in a sec and we'll chat."

Olivia nodded and disappeared into the bathroom. Behind the closed door the water ran.

Sitting beside John on the sofa, Zee dug back into the bags. She whipped out a bottle of prescription medication and handed it to him.

Sertraline—fifty milligrams. Prescribed to Zoey Howard.

"How did you get this?" he wondered.

"There's a hospital about fifteen minutes away. I went to the emergency room. Told the doctor I was on vacation visiting family and forgot my meds for my anxiety disorder. He prescribed five days' worth. I convinced him to bump it up from three, enough to get me through the holidays until I go back home."

She was brilliant. He was so thankful, he could kiss her, but he knew well enough not to.

John popped the lid off and swallowed one dry.

She opened his hand and shook four of those gummies into his palm. Double what she'd given Olivia.

"What is it?"

"Melatonin." She showed him the label on the container. "It'll help you rest but won't make you drowsy when you wake. Trust me."

It was the same stuff his body made. He desperately needed sleep, but he was still a bit wired, and he did trust her. He threw them in his mouth and chewed the fruity gummies.

"And there's this." She gave him a brown paper bag. "Chicken soup, a couple of soft baked rolls and a large salad. There's also a grilled chicken sandwich."

Danger was circling them, and she'd gone out of her way—left her daughter who she hadn't seen in months, who had a ton of questions and must be scared, confused—just to take care of him.

Emotion swamped him, backing up in his chest.

"Eat." She patted his leg and stood, grabbing two of the shopping bags. "I'm going to talk with Olivia."

He cleared his throat. "I told her about Alaska. She asked. I hope that was okay."

She nodded. "I've never told her where I was, thinking it was safer for her, but she's been curious. Now that I can't go back there, it's fine." She walked toward the bathroom.

"Hey" he said, and she stopped, throwing him a glance over her shoulder. "Thanks, Zee." He held up the bag of food and the meds.

Her mouth lifted and the smile was worth a thousand of anyone else's, the look in her eyes he could only describe as affection. She had seen him sweating, frustrated, angry, in the throes of a panic attack. At his worst. No matter how he had been, it never seemed to faze her, other than her showing concern. She always looked at him exactly the same way. Without pity. Only fondness.

Even though he wished it were more than that, he'd take it.

"No problem," she said. "You would've done the same for me. That's what friends are for."

Friends. The word still cut like a dagger in his chest.

Was he a selfish, greedy jerk for feeling this way?

She knocked on the bathroom door, waited for the go-ahead and slipped inside with her daughter.

John took off his boots, scarfed down his food and sucked back another bottle of water. By the time he was done, and his anxiety medicine was kicking in, the ladies emerged from the bathroom that was right next to the bedroom area.

Olivia wore rainbow, doughnut, sunshine pajamas that seemed a stark contrast to their situation. Zee had her arm wrapped around her daughter's shoulder and got her into bed under the covers. "John, why don't you take a hot shower and change your clothes before you go to sleep."

The idea was more than appealing. "I don't have anything to change into."

"I bought you some things. It's all in the bathroom."

One surprise after another with her.

In the bathroom on the counter, he found a cheap men's travel case. The kind you could pick up at any drugstore. Inside there were shaving cream, a razor, deodorant, toothpaste, toothbrush, all the essentials. Zee was used to seeing him clean-shaven. As a SEAL, he'd sported a beard for years, which helped him to blend in while in countries where American servicemen might not be welcome. Once he was discharged, he figured it was time for a fresh, new look.

On top of the closed toilet seat were new clothes, neatly folded. She'd gotten something called the Mission Jean. High-tech pants that were water-resistant, provided four-way stretch and had classic jean styling. There was a pullover sweater with thermal insulation and a performance T-shirt to wear underneath. Boxer briefs. Socks. There was also a pair of sweats. She'd thought of everything.

On the other side of the door, it was quiet enough for him to overhear them talking.

"Are you going to stop stalling and tell me now, Mom?"

"Tell you what, honey?"

"Who is that man?"

"John? He's a friend of mine."

"Like Hunter, Gage and Dean?"

A lot of names. How many men did she have in her life?

Zee gave a soft chuckle. "Those guys are family. Think of them as uncles. John is different. He's... special to me."

"Do you work with him?" Olivia asked.

"No, honey. He was in the military. John is a war hero."

"Wow, really?"

Well, he hadn't described himself as such and neglected to tell Zee about any awards or commendations he'd received. What did any of it mean in the great scheme of things?

"I think so," Zee said. "He would never admit it because he's too humble, but the one thing I know for certain is that he's my hero. Our hero. He's a good person, the best kind, and we can trust him to help us. Okay?"

"Okay, Mom. I like him. He's nice."

His heart stuttered as John smiled to himself. On a deeply personal level, it was important to him what Olivia thought of him. But he was also painfully aware that neither Zee nor her daughter would be in his life for much longer.

He turned on the faucet to shave and give them privacy. Eavesdropping wasn't something he normally did, and he wouldn't make it a new habit.

A shave and shower made him feel like a new man. The medication had a lot to do with it, as well as the hot water sluicing down his body, and getting clean. Worked wonders. He tried on all the clothes but opted to sleep in the sweats for comfort. Probably why she had bought them, thinking the same.

No woman had ever shopped for him before. Dressing in the clothes that Zee had picked out for him was intimate. Nice. He even enjoyed the scent of the bodywash she'd chosen, sandalwood. It had a woodsy warmth. This was something he could get used to, but he shoved the thought aside along with the feeling, tamping them deep down.

John switched off the bathroom light and eased the door open, trying not to make any noise in case the little girl was asleep.

Zee was singing a song about a honey bunny while massaging a pressure point on Olivia's forehead.

John crept out of the bathroom. His gaze met Zee's and he gestured that he was going to the sofa.

"I'll be over in a minute," Zee whispered.

He was surprised to see that she had pulled out the sofa for him. Then again, doing so after Olivia fell asleep might wake her. One additional lovely touch he noted, a rubber wedge-shaped stopper was under the motel door. Ten times better than a flimsy chain.

Zee did think of everything.

Sitting on the bed, he leaned against the back of the sofa and stretched out his legs. His injury didn't ache, which was a good sign. They might have a spot of peace tonight.

Once the singing stopped, the lamp beside the king-size bed was switched off, and Zee came into the sitting area.

"Is she asleep?" he asked.

"Soon, I hope," she said, keeping her voice low. She sat on the edge of the pullout next to his legs and folded her hands in her lap.

"I need the full story. Unredacted. Start with Ryker. Who is he?"

"He's the devil." She flicked a glance at Olivia and lowered her head. "I can't get into details, give you what you want, the unredacted truth. Not while she's in earshot. Always assume a tween is listening even if they look sound asleep."

"I know a safe place where we can go tomorrow. An old friend. Former SEAL." Being around him could be a potential trigger, bringing John to seven out of seven strikes, but now he had his meds. "We can talk there and sort out your next step."

Zee hesitated, and the uncertainty in her face niggled at him.

"She changes everything," he whispered, gesturing to the child across the room. "Please, let me do that much for you."

Another long moment of deliberation. "Okay," she said with a nod. "You're right." She met his gaze and all he wanted was to hold her, assure her that he'd do his best to keep them both safe. "Get some sleep."

As she stood, a horrible thought struck him and he grabbed her hand, stopping her. "You won't take off in the middle of the night with the kid, will you? Disappear on me?" That wasn't the reason she'd given him the melatonin, was it?

She frowned and squeezed his fingers. "No, I won't."

"You give me your word? We'll talk someplace safe before you make any big, life-altering decisions."

A sad smile ghosted her lips. "Not everyone is as honorable as you. A lot of people would break their word."

"Not you. Not with me." He had to believe that at least their friendship was real and if it was, then she would keep her word.

"I wouldn't do that to you, John. I'll tell you everything before I make any big decisions." She squeezed his hand tighter. "I owe you that much. More. I give you my word."

Chapter Ten

Two was lucky he was dead. Otherwise, Ryker would've killed him. Which would have been bad for morale. Whenever he killed someone from his own team the others invariably considered going AWOL.

According to the others, John Lowry had fired the fatal shot.

Ironic.

Bet Two thought Lowry was a problem now as he burned in hell.

More men dead and another dead end. They'd learned of Zee's Zoey Howard alias. But by the time they'd connected it to the prescription filled for sertraline, they'd gotten to the pharmacy too late.

"Did you pick up anything on CCTV that might indicate where the target is?" Ryker asked, taking off his leather coat and tossing it on a chair in the room at the Rainier Inn on the Lewis-McChord joint base.

"The analyst at Langley lost them once they exited I-90. Couldn't find anything useful after that. If they're holed up in a hotel somewhere, they must be using cash or fake IDs."

Damn it. He'd been so close to getting his hands

on his daughter and putting a bullet in Zee he'd tasted victory in his mouth. Now they were in the wind. With Lowry.

The former SEAL had thrown his arms around Ryker's child and his woman. Deep down, he would always think of Zenobia as his, though he'd preferred her young, naive and easy to keep under his thumb. The image of Lowry ushering them out the doors of the academy, facilitating their escape, filled his mind. Dominated everything.

A slow-burning fury coursed in Ryker's veins. But he had to be careful. When it came to Zee, he often let his rage and lust cloud his thinking.

All he had to do was keep his head clear and use the resources at his disposal. Then he'd find her and his daughter. Lowry, too. "We need to extract all the data on her laptop and have it analyzed."

"Seven started the process," Fifteen said, "but he didn't get a chance to finish because we pinpointed the location of the girl and dropped everything to get to her first."

Little good it had done them. If only he had wounded Zee or Lowry at the very least, then it might have been worth the sacrifice of manpower.

Now Seven was dead, too. Killed by the police at the academy. His men were dropping like flies. Given enough time, they could be replaced with more hired guns from the contracted security firm, but the clock was ticking and the loss of his one techie hurt.

"This isn't my specialty, sir, but I'm doing my best." Fifteen clacked away at the keyboard.

"Unfortunately, your best isn't good enough," Ryker said, stating a fact. "Contact our Langley analyst and give them whatever information they need to patch into this laptop and take control of it. They can do the extraction remotely." An expert touch was required to handle this. "I want to know precisely what Zenobia was interested in and looking at besides my daughter. She didn't breach the CIA database for nothing. If she found anything valuable, she'd do something with the information. I need to know what, who, why and where. Then we can figure out her next step."

"How do you know she won't just lie low until she finds a new safe house?" Three asked.

That would be too easy. Instead of playing it safe, Zee preferred to play with fire. Only Ryker wanted to be the one to burn her. "Because I know her too well. She waited months to access the database. According to that dead geek at the hackerspace, she'd found something big. Important to her. Whatever it is, she won't drop it. If she uncovered a loose thread, she'll be compelled to pull it."

Chapter Eleven

A tendril of doubt snaked through Zee.

This is not a mistake. At least that was what she told herself as they drove past the welcome to Montana sign.

They'd gotten an early start, hitting the road at four in the morning after having breakfast at the IHOP down the street. As they had sat in the vinyl booth, the three of them together, eating eggs and sausage and stacks of pancakes, it had felt normal and for five minutes she'd forgotten they were on the run.

With Olivia in the backseat of the car, it was impossible for her and John to discuss the things weighing on either of their minds.

She still couldn't believe that Ryker was leading the Delta team.

He'd told her… *The CIA can't protect you forever. One day, I'll make you regret leaving me.*

She rubbed her arms at the sudden chill that had pebbled her skin.

No matter how this ended, she would never regret getting free of him or keeping Olivia away from that monster.

If he wanted her daughter, he'd have to kill Zee first. But that was the reason he was out there tracking her, wasn't it? To put a bullet in her head.

Out of all the twisted psychos the Agency could have sent. Why had they picked him? Someone who would take pleasure in her death.

This was personal. For both of them.

Zee didn't know what to do. Which choice was wrong? Which was right?

Her daughter was the most important thing, but Zee's decisions also affected John and the rest of Team Topaz. The situation was too big, too monumental to screw it up.

Taking a day to catch her breath at John's friend's place and talking it over with John was a good call. It wasn't a mistake.

But if that was true, then why didn't she believe it? Why did she have a knot twisting in her stomach that in making this choice, there would be repercussions? Something bad was going to happen.

"Are you okay?" John asked, glancing at her.

She forced a smile. "Yeah."

His mouth twitched like he didn't believe her.

"I'm worried," she admitted and glanced back at Olivia, who was reading a book. Zee could never read in a car. It always gave her motion sickness. "Your friend doesn't know we're coming. On Christmas Eve no less." John didn't have his cell phone and didn't have his friend's number memorized. "There are people who wouldn't take kindly to unexpected visitors turning up on their doorstep, two of which are strangers, looking for a place to crash. Correction, hide out from dangerous people."

"Mike isn't *people*. He's…" John shrugged. "Mike. He won't turn us away."

"How can you be sure?" With Delta team out there, time was working against them and she couldn't begin to think about her next step until Olivia was someplace safe. She needed John's idea to pan out.

"We were swim buddies in BUD/S training. Any idea what that is?" John asked.

"I watched a miniseries about the Navy SEAL training course," she said. Looked grueling.

"You were a Navy SEAL?" Olivia looked up from the pages, setting the book down in her lap.

"Yep, kiddo. But once a SEAL, always a SEAL."

"Okay, so he was your swim buddy. So what?" Zee asked.

"In BUD/S, your swim buddy has to be within three feet of you at all times for six months. Two Is One. One Is None. I'm talking everywhere, during an evolution, the ocean, chow hall, running an errand, in the head."

"What's the head?" Olivia asked.

John cleared his throat. "The bathroom. Sorry about that."

"So you mean," Olivia said, "you two were together in the shower and even when doing private stuff?"

"We were very close in BUD/S. Leaving your swim buddy was a serious no-no. Your teammate, your team is everything. No man left behind. Ever.

Dead or alive. But it took both of us about four or five months to internalize the deeper message."

Olivia leaned forward, completely engrossed at this point. "Which was?"

"SEALs are unprotected and vulnerable if we're caught alone in an operation." He cast Zee a glance and she knew this message was also for her. "By working in pairs in training it taught us that we would always be better protected and more likely to succeed in our goals." His gaze shifted back to the road. "We made it through Hell Week together. In some regards, it's the hardest part of training."

"Why?" Olivia asked. "What's so hard about it?"

"The pace is relentless. Downright brutal. Five days and five nights solid with a maximum total of four hours of sleep while doing obstacle courses, beach runs, surf drills, night swims, log PT."

Olivia's eyes were wide with interest. "What's log PT?"

"That's when you do physical training, in boots, long pants and T-shirts, while carrying a telephone pole," he said, eliciting a *sheesh* from Olivia that Zee echoed in her head. "We had to hold it up over heads and do sprints, squats, whatever we were told."

"Sounds excruciating," Zee said. Her training with the CIA to work in the field as a member of Team Topaz had been tough but paled in comparison.

"I've been through worse." His tone was casual, light, masking painful, dark things that she longed for him to share with her when they were in private. "Anyway, we'd made it through Hell Week. We were in the third phase of training and had just finished a two-mile swim that had a seventy-five-minute cut-off. Mike had failed. By seconds."

Olivia grimaced. "Oh, no."

"Who are you telling?" John chuckled. "I had to do the darn thing over with him. Right then and there."

"Did he pass the second time?" Olivia asked before Zee could.

"Yes."

Her daughter exhaled in relief.

"But then we had the next evolution. We had to run an obstacle course."

Zee turned to John. "Without proper rest first?"

He nodded. "That was BUD/S. So, Mike was throwing a fit, feeling sorry for himself. I could see him starting to go down the spiral of self-doubt. He'd already decided in his head that he was going to be too tired to make it. So I pulled him to the side and do you know what I told him?"

"What?" Zee and Olivia asked in unison.

"I said, man, if I asked any yahoo in town to do what you just accomplished, swimming those two miles twice, do you think they would've done it? Think they would've passed at all? You passed and you're feeling sorry for yourself because you're completely wiped? This is the wrong place for sympathy. Because I was right there with you. I'm going to run that obstacle course at your side. Don't wallow, man. Relish it. Relish the fact that you rose to the occasion doing something that ninety-five percent of the global population would run from, much less try. Relish the fact that you won a battle that most people lose—the battle with themselves. I told him, man, we got this. And he passed."

"Because you helped him," Olivia said with a bright smile. "Was that the moment when you understood the point of having a swim buddy?"

"It sure was. We both did. By the end of BUD/S we could finish each other's sentences and almost shared a brain." He chuckled. "We each know that we can count on the other when we need them most. That's how I'm sure he'll help us."

John knew how to deliver a speech and tell a story. She'd give him that. He truly was compelling, even to Olivia. "Fine. I'm convinced Mike will help us, but is he married?"

He frowned. "Yeah. He's on his third wife. Enola Littlewolf."

Zee folded her arms. "How do you know that she'll let us in?"

"All right, you've got me there. But Mike is persuasive and she's awesome. I met her at their wedding right before I moved to Alaska."

If Mike was anything like John, Enola was probably wrapped around his finger.

Zee's heart fluttered at the thought of being in a relationship with John, and how there would be nothing that she wouldn't do for him. Squeezing her thighs together, she pushed the thought aside.

Thanks to light traffic they pulled up sooner than she expected in front of the two-story house that sat on a large plot of land and offered sweeping views of rolling hills, evergreens and mountains.

The house was decked out for the holidays with a

ton of string lights, wreaths hung on every window; several lanterns were around the door and an animated Santa sleigh and reindeer sat in the front yard.

"Wait here." John hopped out of the car, climbed up the front porch and knocked.

He looked great in the new clothes she'd bought him. Stylish. They flattered his body, those long legs and all that sexy muscle.

Zee cracked the window, figuring with luck that she might be able to overhear the conversation.

"What are we going to do if they don't let us stay?" Olivia asked.

Zee had no clue. She'd probably have to abandon the idea of following up on her lead and investigating further into what went wrong on her team's mission. Doing it with her daughter in tow wasn't a possibility.

"We'll figure it out, honey. I don't want you to worry about it."

The front door opened. A guy just as big as John stepped out. Six-three. A solid two hundred pounds. A tighter, cleaner haircut. Black curly hair.

The two men hugged, and it was evident that Mike was thrilled to see him, but Zee couldn't hear a word exchanged.

When Mike gestured for him to enter, John hiked his thumb back at the car. His friend glanced over and nodded at John's explanation. The smile fell from Mike's face as he shut the front door and stepped out onto the porch.

She had to trust John's judgment. Surely he would let his friend know about the possibility of danger following them, but hopefully, he'd limit the details and neglect to mention the CIA at all.

"Hooyah!" Mike said, slapping John on the back.

John turned to the car, flashing a grin that made her belly tighten, and waved them over.

"See, Mom. John was right."

He'd already managed to turn her daughter into his cheerleader in less than twenty-four hours. *Impressive.*

But Zee noticed that Mike hadn't gone into the house and cleared it with his new wife. She swallowed the comment, not wanting to tempt fate.

She rolled up the window, shut off the engine and they grabbed their bags.

On the porch, John took the duffel from her. "Mike Cutler, this is Zee and her daughter, Olivia."

Smiling, she was pleased that John hadn't offered her surname. A good indication he'd only shared the necessary details with his friend.

"Pleasure to meet you." Mike gave her a double handshake with his left cupping the back of her right. "Olivia, I'd say you were about my daughter's age. Let me guess, eleven?"

Olivia grinned. "I'll be eleven tomorrow."

"Oh," Mike said, beaming. "A Christmas birthday. That's pretty special."

"We call it Olivmas," her daughter said.

Mike touched his nose. "That's clever. I love it. Come in." He opened the door wide.

As they walked into the house, the smell of eucalyptus and sugar cookies hit them. It was warm and comfy and loud. Kids ranging in age from eleven to, she guessed, twenty were running around all over the place.

A soaring Christmas tree that hit the ten-foot ceiling engulfed a corner. Wrapped gifts with red bows were piled underneath it.

Mike closed the door. "We're a blended family. Enola's got three boys from her previous marriage. I've got two boys from my first. Another boy and girl from my second. Amanda is the youngest. She'll be happy to have another girl around, Olivia. I can assure you of that. The kids are with our exes on Thanksgiving and we both have them together for Christmas. So, it's a crazy full house. But you're more than welcome to stay. After lunch, we're heading into town for the winter carnival. We do it every Christmas Eve. It's a ton of fun."

Two boys on the sofa playing video games started roughhousing and overturned the coffee table.

"Knock it off!" Mike said. "And clean up that mess."

"Yes, sir," the two said in unison.

"Amanda!" Mike called out.

A girl with curly dark hair who favored Mike came to the top of the stairs. "What?"

"Don't *what* me," Mike said.

Amanda frowned. "Yes, sir, what can I do for you, oh mighty one?"

"That's better." Mike put a hand to Olivia's back and pushed her forward. "This is Olivia. This is her mom, Mrs...." He glanced between her and John. "Is it Lowry? You've been best man at all three of my weddings—if you got hitched without me there, man—"

"Just call me Zee. Let's keep it casual."

"And say hi to your uncle John," Mike said.

Amanda waved. "Hey, Uncle John. Hi, Zee."

"Make Olivia feel welcomed. She's sharing your room since there's no place else. John and Zee will bunk in the attic."

John stiffened, making her wonder what the attic was like. A dusty space with no drywall and exposed insulation?

Safe shelter was all that mattered to her, and if Olivia had a bed to share, then Zee would be fine on the floor.

"Cool," Amanda said. "Come on up, Olivia. We'll hang in my room until lunch."

Olivia looked back at Zee for the okay.

"Go have fun."

Olivia took off up the stairs, hauling her backpack.

"Where's Enola?" John asked, glancing around.

"In the kitchen." Mike flashed a tight smile. "Let me show you the attic first." He hurried to the stairs. "Get you settled in. Don't worry, Zee, it's cozy up there."

They climbed two flights of stairs, passed a small hallway bathroom, and he opened the door, letting Zee and John in first.

A window on the far wall let in natural light. In front of it was a full-size bed with a nightstand to the side. Was the bed even a full? It looked more like an oversize twin, large enough for a teenage boy to fit comfortably. Alone.

A surge of alarm rippled through her.

"You two will have your privacy away from everyone," Mike said, easily. "You stayed up here during the wedding, didn't you, John?"

"About us sharing," John said, his cheeks turning redder than strawberries, "this one room—"

Zee put a hand on his forearm. "It'll be just fine." If they handled a sleeping bag, surely this would be nothing, but even at the slight touch on his arm sexual awareness simmered between them, and she stepped away, dropping her hand. It would be easier, if John wasn't quite so hot, say hideous as a troll, or stupid. Stupid wasn't attractive. Neither was mean, and he wasn't that either. In fact, he was ridiculously good-looking, wise, funny, brave, patient, resourceful—everything she'd ever wanted in a man. *Damn near perfect.* "Thank you so much for letting us stay. Considering the circumstances."

"Think nothing of it," Mike said. "John's my brother in every sense but blood. Whatever you two need is yours. I'm happy to help."

"I'd love to meet Enola," she said.

"Plenty of time for that. Get cleaned up. Catch your breath. Give me a chance to grease the wheels with her. Then come down to the kitchen. Be sure not to mention the words *fugitive* or *dangerous*. When it comes to discussing specifics, less is more, but I'll do my best to prevent the question mill from running wild."

The shooting at the school would make the news

and be splashed across social media, but names wouldn't be given, and pictures of students wouldn't be shown. The CIA would do what they could to clean up the stories and filter information.

"Lunch is going to be soon. I can't wait to get the kids out of the house and to the carnival, so they can burn off some energy." Mike gave them an exasperated look, then he was out of the room and shutting the door.

John set the duffel bag down. "I can sleep on one of the sofas downstairs. I'm sure no one will mind. You don't have to be cooped up in here with me."

"If we can share a sleeping bag without clothes, I think we can handle a bed with us both fully dressed." They were two mature adults capable of controlling themselves.

Turning, she looked away from the bed to John and her confidence faltered.

A flash of disappointment, maybe even hurt, crossed his face when he closed his eyes, as if to block her words. It only lasted a heartbeat.

Then John stepped closer, right up to her, and she wrestled the reflex to back away. Looming over her, he stilled, his face turning deadpan, making him suddenly appear as placid as she struggled to feel. On an inhale, she took in a lungful of sandalwood spice and the luscious base note that was pure John.

The scintillating proximity to him had her heart and body warring with her mind. Never had she felt such a powerful craving for anyone or anything in her life. She didn't want to desire someone the way she wanted him.

Maybe when it came to falling for someone, choice wasn't a factor.

Cupping her jaw, he tilted her head back. His gaze searched hers before landing on her mouth. Every cell filled with the impulse to touch him, to kiss him. The way she was drawn to this man felt like fate and resisting it went against the laws of nature.

He slid a finger behind her earlobe, and her answering bone-deep shiver sent tingles to her thighs.

"Whatever you want, *buddy*," he said.

The little word dissolved, leaving behind a bitter sting.

It was so silly. Buddy, friend, none of it should faze her since she was the one who had erected this platonic wall between them.

Part of her wondered what the point was of pretending any longer. No matter how much she pushed him away, tried to protect him, he kept inserting himself between her and danger, rushing to her side to help her without asking for anything in return. He was the most selfless, bighearted man she knew.

A lump of frustration formed in her throat as she looked up at him.

Dropping his hand, he went to the door. "I'm going for a walk." His voice was gravelly with heat, so rough it scored her like sandpaper. "I need to stretch my legs. Get some air." And he was gone.

She considered running after him, stopping him, but there was so much he didn't know about her. Things in her past that could change how he felt, how he looked at her.

It was complicated and messy. At the heart of it

was Ryker. Thinking about what she'd gone through with him filled her with such shame. The fact that she had fallen for Ryker in the beginning…what did that say about her judgment?

But she wouldn't let her embarrassment over her past mistakes stop her from telling John the truth. She owed him nothing less.

Maybe he would understand. She loved the way he saw the world. How he appreciated complexity, and even in ugly things he could find beauty.

After composing herself, she checked her appearance in the bathroom mirror. The shower in the hall bath was small and the sloping ceiling was so low John would probably have to hunch over inside. She finger-combed her curls into submission and dabbed on lip gloss.

On the way to the kitchen, she smiled at the kids she passed, and they acknowledged her with a head nod or wave.

The two oldest ones were clearly Mike's. Tall and strapping with curly dark hair. He must have been around their age, maybe a little older when he had them.

At the threshold of the kitchen, she spotted Mike. He was standing behind a dark-haired woman who was in front of the stove. His arms were wrapped around her waist. He whispered in her ear and kissed her neck.

The woman giggled. "Stop it, Mike. I already said it's fine."

A persuasive sweet talker who could bend his woman to his will.

As Mike kissed her again, pressing his pelvis to her behind, Zee considering backing away to give them privacy, but Mike glanced over his shoulder, spotting her.

He waved her in with a wide grin, stepped to the side, and looked at his wife. "Hey, babe, this is Zee."

Enola spun around from the stove and wiped her hands on dish towel. "Hi, I'm Enola. It's so nice to meet you."

Zee extended her hand, but Enola gave her a big hug instead. It was warm and genuine and much appreciated.

Enola was a pretty woman with voluptuous curves and a smile like sunshine that immediately put Zee at ease. Her hair was straight and black, falling to her waist in a glossy sheet.

"What can I do to help?" Zee looked around the kitchen at the feast that was being prepared.

"Oh, nothing." Enola waved a dismissive hand. "I've got it under control."

Never one to shy away from pitching in when there was work to be done, Zee went to the sink and washed her hands. "Tell me what to do. I insist. Carve the turkey? Mash those boiled potatoes? Slice the ham?"

Enola grinned, the gratefulness in her eyes unmistakable while Mike leaned against the counter drinking a bottle of beer with a hand on his hip.

"All of the above," Enola said. "Please." She opened the oven and took out macaroni and cheese and put green beans in a serving dish.

Mike tipped the bottle back, taking another swig

of beer. "Oh, John said not to wait for him to eat lunch. After that car ride, he needs a long walk to stretch out the kinks."

A sharp pang twisted through her chest. He needed a long walk away from her.

"I will leave you lovely ladies to it." Mike disappeared into the next room and yelled at the boys.

"Men," Enola muttered under her breath. "Useless in the kitchen, right?"

Perhaps Mike was, but John was a great cook. He enjoyed whipping up meals, elevating tasty improvisation into an art form. Which probably explained why he wasn't much for baking. That was more of a science.

"Well, I'm happy to help," Zee said, deciding it was better not to comment. She picked up the carving knife that was next to the turkey and got to work.

Enola started frosting a cake. "I heard we have a birthday tomorrow."

"Olivia is turning eleven."

"Does she like yellow cake with chocolate frosting?"

"Loves it." Olivia had never been a picky eater, but she wasn't partial to lemon-flavored sweets.

"Always a winner, am I right? Unless some kid has a food allergy. They're all allergic to something these days. Nuts. Gluten. Dairy. Fresh air." She sighed. "I was thinking we could save this cake for tomorrow since I've got cookies and pies. I could add some sprinkles to the top of the cake and put her name on it. We've got candles tucked away in a drawer somewhere."

Tears stung Zee's eyes at Enola's kindness. "That's really sweet of you."

Emotions welled in her chest. Remorse over the deadly situation she'd dragged Olivia and John into. Fear that Ryker would get his hands on her daughter. Guilt for robbing her little girl of normalcy and stability, forcing her to grow up far too fast. Regret over hurting John by pushing him away when all she wanted was to pull him closer. To love him.

And it hit her like a lightning bolt.

I love John.

The timing was all wrong. Disastrous.

Doubts, concerns, worries—stacked up in a long list of reasons why they shouldn't be together.

Professionally, she took risks all the time and convinced others to step into that dark void of the unknown with her, all while suppressing what she needed on a personal level. But she was so tired of denying that she needed John. That she cared for him. Loved him. As much more than a friend.

A tear leaked from her eye and she sniffled.

Enola came to her side, handing her a tissue. "It's just a cake. No trouble at all. It was already baked, and I was going to ice it anyway."

"But it'll mean the world to Olivia." A stranger thought of a birthday cake for her daughter while Zee was plotting how to get evidence that might prove the innocence of her team. What kind of life was she giving Olivia? "And I appreciate it. Thank you." She dabbed at her eyes. "I feel like such a bad mother." The absolute worst. She hadn't even thought of buying cupcakes from a gas station convenience store.

Enola glanced around like she had a secret to share before opening a cabinet above the wall oven. She pushed some stuff around, pulled out a bottle of Lillet Rose, and poured a couple of ounces of the aperitif into two glasses over rocks, topped it with seltzer.

"It's five o'clock somewhere." She handed Zee a glass. "The only mother who has never felt like a failure or that she wasn't getting it quite right at some point was Mother Teresa." They both laughed. "If any woman ever tells you different, she's a liar. Take comfort in that." She rubbed Zee's back and clinked their glasses together. "Cheers."

Zee sipped the bittersweet drink that tasted of berries and orange blossoms. Enola's pep talk relieved a bit of the pressure that had been simmering inside her chest.

"Are you guys going to join us for the winter carnival?" Enola added milk and butter to the potatoes.

"John and I have some important things to discuss."

"No need to say another word. How about after lunch, we take Olivia with us. Mike always makes the kids buddy up whenever we go somewhere. Even at the mall. Two Is One, One Is None," Enola said, imitating him, and Zee smiled, understanding the significance. "I'm sure she and Amanda will be glued at the hip, but I'll keep a close eye on her so you won't need to worry. It's a lot of fun. I guarantee she'll enjoy herself."

Mike and Enola were a godsend. A holiday activity with kids around her own age was exactly what Olivia needed. A healthy distraction, a slice of normal.

Zee could use a bit of that herself. "That'd be great and I'll take care of cleaning up the dishes."

"You don't have to do that. You're our guest."

"I insist. That way you guys can get going sooner, which I think Mike would prefer."

"We both would." Enola took another sip of her drink.

Coming here had been a good decision. Not a mistake.

Once again, John was right.

Chapter Twelve

The long walk across the property had done John good, allowed him the distance to get his head straight. Zee had him spinning in circles, on the verge of his control snapping and being completely destroyed. He despised the sensation.

On his way back, he'd caught sight of Mike's GMC Yukon XL heading out down the road. The vehicle looked packed to the brim. He wondered if Zee had been in the car, or if she was waiting for him back at the house to talk through her situation. Come up with a way forward.

She was all about business and maintaining the lines in the sand. Of course, she'd be at the house. Looking lovelier and more tempting than ever. Ready to discuss a plan.

But he was going to be hands-off with her this time. Just touching Zee's jaw earlier in the attic had been too much. He had silently commanded his heart to keep beating, his lungs to continue pumping air. Knowing what her naked body felt like against his, those spectacular curves—warm, silky skin and toned limbs, yet, with a woman's softness—was miles beyond anything his self-control could deal with again sleeping in a bed next to her. Clothes or no clothes.

Entering the house, he removed his coat.

"I'm in the kitchen," Zee called out when he let the door slam shut.

He walked through the living room and down the hall.

Zee was cleaning the kitchen, loading the dishwasher and wiping down counters with all the precision and focus she applied to everything else.

He drank in the sight of her with such extreme pleasure that his blood pressure shot so high he could actually hear it rushing in his ears.

"Hi." She glanced back at him over her shoulder. Heartbreakingly beautiful. Then she flashed one of those tentative smiles, sweet vulnerability in her eyes, and it hit him in the solar plexus, knocking the air from his lungs. "I made a plate for you and put it in the microwave. Are you hungry?" Her slightly husky voice, the softness of it, stroked over him, making his gut clench.

"Starved." He went to the microwave and grabbed the food. "Thanks."

Sitting down at the table with his back to her, he dug into the meal. She'd prepared his plate exactly as he would've done for himself. A mix of white- and dark-meat turkey, one slice of ham, mashed potatoes sans gravy, a little mac and cheese and lots of veggies. No sweet potatoes smothered in marshmallows.

It pleased and pained him that she knew him so well.

"Everyone left a little while ago," she said. "They all piled into the SUV and somehow seemed to fit. Olivia made fast friends with Amanda."

"Of course, she did. She's like you."

Behind him, he heard her movements stop. Felt her gaze on the back of his neck.

"I'll take that as a compliment," she said in a low, unsure voice.

"You should. It was meant as one." He stuffed his mouth full of more food, happy to have a home-cooked meal after the past two days. "I gave it some thought and it's best if I use the sleeping bag. I can put it out on the floor at the foot of the bed." There was just enough room to make it work. "Gives you some space in the bed and keeps me from being in anyone's way downstairs."

The best thing was to keep his distance from her. Sharing a bed would only complicate matters, especially when he needed to stay on his toes to make sure she didn't get any deeper under his skin.

"John... I thought...it wouldn't be a problem for us to share the bed. Do you really think this is necessary?"

He'd finally found a woman he wanted to give himself to, entirely, and he had the misfortune of her not wanting him in return. She was a constant source of temptation for him and he was at his breaking point of resistance.

"Yes. It's necessary." For the sake of his sanity if nothing else. He finished his food and took the plate to the sink.

"Fine," she said with a sharp note of determination that made him sigh. "But I'll take the sleeping bag. You can have the bed."

What was this new game she wanted to play?

She sucked in a deep breath, standing there like she was waiting for a response from him.

But everything he wanted to say, everything he needed to tell her, got stuck in his throat. He didn't want to argue, try to convince her, he simply wanted her. Even though it struck him as wrong to desire more than friendship, and the truth was, they were friends. Best friends.

Why couldn't that be enough for him?

Zee marched out of the kitchen and he heard her footsteps ascending the stairs.

He put the plate in the dishwasher, thinking everything over, questions burning through his head that begged for answers.

Friendship wasn't enough because from the moment they'd first met there had been an instant flare of attraction. At least on his part. But all those hours they'd spent in his house, all the lunches, dinners, lingering looks, stolen touches, long conversations late into the night enticed him to believe she might be interested, too.

Still, he'd put his desires and expectations in check until she had kissed him in that cabin.

The kiss had not only filled his head with possibilities that burned straight through him, tightening in his groin, but also the way she'd kissed him had been flirty, fiery. Filthy.

Not the least bit friendly.

The genie was out of the bottle and there was no way to put it back in.

Leaving the kitchen, he strode through the house and took the stairs two at a time up to the attic.

She was on her knees rolling out the sleeping bag at the foot of the bed. "If you think this is best, then this is the way it's going to work. It's my sleeping bag and your friend's house after all."

He stepped inside the room and closed the door. "Let's forget about what's *best* for a minute, or what's right or wrong, and discuss what's real."

Her gaze flew up to his as she sat back on her heels. "What do you mean?"

"You know everything of importance about me while you've still got all these secrets. Are you going to be honest with me? Answer everything that I ask truthfully?"

"Yes." Nodding, she climbed to her feet. "I promised that I would. Whatever you want to know, ask me."

"The kiss." Actually, kisses. The cabin and the airport. "Did it mean more to you or was it really only a gesture of friendship?"

Looking him in the eye, she backed away, putting distance between them, and his heart sank. He'd committed to helping her and he'd follow through, but it hurt to think that things were only platonic for her. He understood of course. Would respect her feelings.

The wall stopped her retreat. "After everything that's transpired, your need for the unredacted truth, and that's your first question?"

"Yep." He folded his arms.

She looked downright flustered. "Why that one above all the others?"

Because it would frame every other answer that came from her mouth. "Humor me, please. I need to know the truth."

Rolling her shoulders as if bracing herself, she met his gaze. "It was more. Much more for me."

Her response only sparked other questions for him.

Not understanding, he sought to close the gap between them and strode toward her.

But she sidestepped his touch.

"Are you afraid of me?" he asked. "Afraid of how I'll react about something?"

"No, I'm not afraid of you. But how can I even think about being close to you, the way I want," she said in a voice that shook slightly, "when there are so many things that you need to know about me." With a grimace, she lowered her head. "I need to put all my cards on the table before you come any closer. Because once I do. You might want to walk out that door."

There was nothing that she could say that would make him turn his back on her. Nothing. Didn't she realize that by now?

"Put them on the table. I'm listening."

She chewed her bottom lip and he saw fear in her eyes.

"You can tell me anything," he said. "No matter how bad. No matter how ugly." His gut twisted hard when she started to tremble.

"You asked me a question in the motel," she said, "that I couldn't answer at the time with Olivia nearby."

He thought for moment. So much had happened. "About Ryker? Who is he?"

She squeezed her eyes shut. "The biggest mistake of my life, who gave me the greatest gift."

John shook his head. "I don't understand."

Looking at him, Zee took another deep breath, letting it out slowly through her mouth. "I told you about my childhood."

"Breezy Point." Insulated. Right wing. How she felt like she didn't quite fit in. "Yeah."

"I rebelled. A lot. I was a constant headache for my dad and source of concern for my mom. In high school, I fell in love with computers and coding. When I went to MIT," she said, referring to the Massachusetts Institute of Technology, "my dad was so relieved, he thought he didn't have to worry about me anymore, that I was on track. Focused. The summer before I was set to complete my degree, I received an encrypted invitation from a hacktivist group in Germany, to come and check them out. I did and got caught up in their cause. They did good things, Robin Hood style, and some not so good things." She ran her fingers back through her hair. "Then I met Ryker. Ryker Rudin."

"In Germany?" he asked.

"Yes." She blew out a heavy breath. "At the time, I didn't know he was CIA and working me to be an asset. He came across as the ultimate bad boy, someone my father would loathe. Fit right in with my rebel-with-a-cause profile. He was charismatic, charming, flattering, and seduced me. Rather easily, thinking back on it. They'd profiled me and told him who he needed to be, how to act, to get close to me. He used me to take the group down and then threatened to have me arrested unless I went to work for the CIA," she said, covering part of her face with one hand, like she was ashamed.

"A common tactic the CIA and FBI use to recruit specialized talent. Not the seduction part, but the rest."

"That wasn't all. Ryker added a caveat to the deal that I had to remain his girlfriend. He claimed it was so the Agency could keep an eye on me at all times and that it was the only way he would endorse me for a position with the CIA instead of having me arrested."

A flash of white-hot anger spiked through him. "He couldn't do that. No one would give him the power, the authority to coerce you like that."

"I know that now. But at the time, I was only nineteen, hadn't the first clue about the CIA's inner workings. I was terrified to go to prison, and the thought of my father never speaking to me again was…" Her voice trailed off as she shook her head.

"How much older was he when this happened?"

"Fifteen years."

It sickened John. To think of a thirty-year-old with someone forty-five didn't seem like a big deal. But at nineteen, she had been too young. Too innocent. Still a teenager.

"Like a naive idiot, I agreed," she said. "I accepted his deal."

He edged closer and this time she didn't move away. "How long were you with him?"

"Two years. Three months. Nine days. At first, our relationship in Virginia had been the way it'd been in Germany and I thought it might be okay. I wanted to believe his words instead of trusting my feelings that there was something wrong with him. But then, slowly, the real Ryker came out. More and more the charming facade fell, and I saw him for the monster that he is. A sociopath, incapable of love." A shudder ripped through her. "It was a nightmare. I honestly thought if I had tried to leave him, he would've killed me and made it look like an accident. He was very good at that. Killing and making it look like a mishap." She hugged herself and rubbed her arms. "*Everything* was on his terms, his way. Even sex. He manipulated me from the very beginning and every day that I was with him." Tears welled in her eyes. "Getting pregnant with Olivia was the biggest deception of all."

Every muscle in John's body locked down as he connected the dots.

Trench Coat—the maniac at the school—was Olivia's father?

Chapter Thirteen

Shock rocked through John, but he didn't let it show as he took another step closer to Zee. "How did Ryker deceive you?"

"I found out that he had been poking holes in the condoms and switched my birth control pills for sugar pills."

"What?" He reeled back horrified, unable to hide his emotions. "What kind of man would do that?" His voice had risen two octaves.

"The despicable, selfish, manipulative kind. Like Ryker Rudin." She wrung her hands and shook her head. "When I was five months pregnant, he proposed. After I refused him, said no, he admitted the truth about the condoms and my pills. Told me that now we would be linked together forever. No matter what. He actually thought, in his twisted head, that once the baby was born, I would forgive him." A tear leaked from the corner of her eye. "I love Olivia and she's the best blessing I could ask for, but what he did to me was…"

He brought her into his arms and held her. "Reprehensible. Unforgivable."

She nodded against his chest. "Hunter Wright, he's my team leader, former anyway. The CIA wanted him to put together a unit to focus on taking out sensitive high-value targets."

"An elimination team, like Delta?" He turned, sitting them both down on the bed.

"Not quite. There are two kinds of teams that work for the Agency. Those like mine are given specialized missions. Agency-acknowledged targets. We limit collateral damage and ensure the assignment never gets traced back to them. When we succeed, we're celebrated in the halls at Langley. Given monetary bonuses for a job well done and a lot of leeway when we're at home. Teams like Delta, they clean up problems. They live and work in the shadows. Operate on American soil as well as abroad. They're expendable. Sometimes they do heinous things to get the job done. Nobody wants to see them or hear about them. The Agency just wants the problem to be gone."

He caressed her face and wiped her tears with his thumbs. "So, Hunter agreed to put together a unit and picked you."

"Exactly. The team was code-named Topaz. He handpicked every member. He saw I was talented and thought that with the right training I would be exceptional in the field. I had turned him down several times before, but when I had learned what Ryker had done, I went to Hunter. Swallowed my shame and spilled my guts, told him everything and agreed to be on his team, if he could get me away from Ryker and protect my child." She curled her arms around her stomach.

John wrapped an arm around her and pulled her close. She felt good pressed up next to him. She smelled good, too, always, but he hated seeing her upset. "How did Hunter respond?"

"Hunter was furious. He found Ryker, and they got into a fight, right in the middle of the cafeteria. Came to blows and drew blood. Afterward, Hunter took me to the director of operations. Spelled out what needed to happen. The director had always hated Ryker, thought he was scum, and agreed. Ryker was sent to work in the shadows, far from Langley where I'd never have to see him, leading cleanup teams. They made it clear to him that if he came near me, my child, or if I so much as got a paper cut that wasn't mission-related, they were going to take care of him."

Reining in his fury over Ryker, John put a supportive hand to her back, processing everything she'd told him. "Until things went sideways for your team."

She propped her elbow on her thigh and pressed her palm to her forehead. "We're good people. We were following orders. I don't know what went wrong."

"Tell me about the mission."

She pinched her lips in a grim line.

"They've seen my face," he said. "There was CCTV all over the school. I'm sure they know my name by now. I'm already in this. Neck-deep."

Pain and tears lingered in her eyes. "I'm so sorry. I never meant to involve you in any of this."

"Don't be sorry. I'm not." He wanted to kiss her, to confess how deeply he felt for her. "Tell me about the mission."

"Do you know who Khayr Faraj is?"

The name had his hardwired instincts snapping to high alert. "Definitely. He's an extremist, a terrorist, with a great deal of power. His number of followers grows each day. He recruits American citizens to carry out attacks in the United States. Pretty soon he'll be a bigger threat than Abu Bakr al-Baghdadi and Osama bin Laden combined. SEALs tried to take him out a couple of times. Hard to do when there are no pictures of him. Only a description. A distinctive birthmark on his cheek, if I recall correctly."

"We were ordered to eliminate Faraj in the mountains of Afghanistan, at a meeting he was supposed to have with his financial backer. A corrupt Afghan official who was secretly funding him."

"Sounds like an op I would've loved to sink my teeth into. I know a bunch of warfare operators who'd say the same."

"We were eager to take him out, too," she said. "Normally, we assess the situation and decide how to best achieve the objective. The strange part about this mission was that we were instructed to use explosives and take out everyone at the meeting. We thought we had been successful. A man with a birthmark on his cheek matching the description we had been given was there, but it turns out that it wasn't Faraj."

"Then who did you kill?"

"A tribal leader who was meeting with the corrupt Afghan official. Neither was a sanctioned target on his own. The official would have been acceptable collateral damage since the meeting with Faraj and exchange of money would've proven his guilt. Without that proof it spelled big trouble with an ally."

Errors of that magnitude weren't common. "How did the mistake happen?"

"I wish I knew. We were in the dark. Still are."

"What did your handler say?" Teams like hers always had a CIA point person.

"We never got a chance to ask. Barely made it out of Afghanistan. Our planned extraction was compromised. A cleanup team ambushed us. They had been waiting. We weren't sure if they were CIA or if someone else had sent them. But Hunter was prepared, as always, and had a contingency ready."

A leader was supposed to take care of his people. The more John heard about Hunter Wright, the more he liked the man.

"We made it back stateside by hiding out for weeks in a shipping container on a freighter. Tight quarters for the four of us, but we made do, toughed it out. Hunter tried to meet up with our CIA handler, but everything went to hell in a handbasket. Instead of Kelly Russell turning up at the meet the way she was supposed to, another cleanup team of mercenaries did. It was a shoot first never ask questions type of debacle. They had no interest in apprehending us and taking us in alive. That's when we knew without a doubt that the CIA wanted to eliminate us. We had to split up and go our separate ways. Stay under the radar."

"How are you all going to clear your names, scattered and on the run?"

She shook her head. "I'm not sure. But I found something a couple of days ago, hacking into the CIA's database."

"Is that how they found you? Because you went nosing around where you shouldn't have?"

"Guilty as charged," she said with a nod. "We were set up, and I can't let this go. Finding the truth is the only way I can have a life with Olivia. She doesn't deserve this."

He took her hand in his. "Neither do you." Falsely accused and on the run with her life in shambles. There was also the complication of her ex, Olivia's father, spearheading the team after Zee.

"I found a lead." There was hesitancy in her eyes.

"But?"

She got up, crossed the room and unzipped her bag, pulling out the sat phone. "I can reach Hunter on this. A one-time, dire-straits call. When he picks up he'll say *parachute*. I have to respond with *rip cord*."

"A security challenge-response authentication?"

"Yes, then I'll receive coordinates and instructions that will eventually get me to him. I have a choice. Leave now. Or follow the lead first. Find out what I can."

John wanted Zee and Olivia to be safe. No matter what. But ultimately, the only way for them to remain safe was for her team to clear their names. "What's the lead?"

"I discovered that right after we were set up, the Agency fired David Bertrand."

"Why is that important?" he wondered.

"Bertrand worked in a support capacity on our last operation. I think he knew something."

"Do you know where he is?"

"He disappeared. I haven't been able to find a trace of him anywhere, but I don't think he's dead. I think he's hiding. He had a fiancée. I was able to locate her. Luisa Morales. From footage I saw of her on CCTV, she looked happy. Not like she was grieving."

"You think they're together?"

"They were so in love. If they're not together, she's the best shot at finding him."

"Where is she?"

"Idaho Falls."

"That's less than a three-hour drive." Felt like providence to him. "We'll go today."

"There's something else. I need to access the internet, but away from here. I left something behind in the CIA's database. A zero-day virus."

"What's that?"

"A Trojan horse program I designed to exploit a software security flaw. It's called zero-day because the CIA has zero chance of plugging the hole. The malware will gather everything related to Team Topaz and anything Bertrand had worked on. I'm positive there's something there. But once I go back into the system to get it—"

"They'll find you."

She nodded.

He rubbed a hand across his jaw. It was a big risk, but it might reap an even bigger reward if it provided information that her team could use to clear their names.

"Olivia will be safe here," he said. "You can access the internet in Idaho Falls. I think we have to take the chance."

But there was still something else he needed to know.

Chapter Fourteen

"Put the analyst on speaker," Ryker said for efficiency. Everyone in the room would be clued in and on the same page.

Only three of his men were present. The rest were taking downtime: sleeping, eating, whatever tickled their fancy so long as it was being done in one of the rooms at the Rainier Inn.

"Delta India here," a female voice said over the encrypted secure line. India was the designation given to the intelligence analyst tasked with field support from Langley. "Ninety percent of the files the target accessed in the home database were in the Topaz folder. But I can't say for certain what she was looking for. Nothing was downloaded."

"Talk to me about the other ten percent," Ryker said.

"She tried to backtrack through the last files that David Bertrand accessed."

"What do you mean tried?"

"She must have realized that she was in danger of getting caught if she stayed online much longer.

She started the process but didn't have time to complete it."

Every detail India gave him he lined up in his head like dominoes, waiting for the right piece to start the chain reaction and knock them all down. "Who is Bertrand?"

"A former analyst. He provided support to her team several times, including their last mission."

The plot thickens. "Where is he?"

"We have no idea. He was fired shortly after Team Topaz was disavowed and a kill order on them was authorized," she said. "He's gone underground. There's no trace of him. Something else you should know. As of 2100 last night, a kill order was issued on Bertrand."

The man had been fired and no one cared diddly-squat about him until Zenobia started sniffing around, digging into him. Now there's a kill order out on him. *Curious.*

Zee would love to know that. It meant whatever thread she found was the right one. Too bad for her, Ryker had no interest in helping her, only killing her and retrieving his daughter.

"What did you find in the dive on her laptop? Was she trying to locate Bertrand?" Ryker asked.

"There wasn't a single query on Bertrand on the computer, but that doesn't mean she didn't try to find him. It looks as if she performed routine scrubs on the hard drive, erasing it every few days. A painstaking precaution. Probably conducted within hours of accessing the internet in the event her place was raided and her laptop seized. She may have tried searching for Bertrand before. There's no way of knowing. But you got lucky that she didn't wipe the hard drive clean the last time."

Luck came in two varieties. The good kind and the bad. At the moment, Ryker wasn't feeling fortunate. The pictures on her laptop had led him to his daughter, only to lose Olivia and confirm that Lowry was still helping Zee.

"Tell me something fortuitous," Ryker demanded. "Or at the very least, useful."

"The target probably hit a dead end trying to locate Bertrand. I did find other queries. She was doing a deep dive into Luisa Morales."

The name didn't ring a bell from the case file he'd been given. "Who is that?"

"Bertrand's fiancée."

This was the piece he'd been waiting for. "Do you have a location for Morales?"

"Idaho Falls. She relocated there after Bertrand was fired."

"Find out exactly where in the city. As much info on her as you can. Contact me when you have it. We'll be en route. You have until we touch down to give me what I need."

"Yes, sir," she said, and he heard typing. "From your current location, your flight time will be approximately four hours."

"Then you have four hours. Don't disappoint me. Also, tell the Agency that I'll handle the kill order on Bertrand." He disconnected after India acknowledged, and turned to his men. "Get the others ready. We leave in twenty minutes."

Chapter Fifteen

There had been so many instances when John had been alone in his house in Alaska, had relaxed his mind, let it wander, and his thoughts had rolled in free-floating directions that invariably, sooner or later, turned to Zee.

Consistent happenstance alone should have made him realize the depths of his feelings for her, but he'd always dismissed it. Had made excuses not to dwell, not to feed it energy. Each time they had gotten together for chess or a meal he'd been a bit dazed, stupefied to inaction.

Sitting beside her in Mike's attic was no different than those other times.

She put a hand on his leg and looked up at him. "You've been incredible. Thank you for helping me get to Olivia before Delta team did. I couldn't have done any of this without you."

All his thoughts and feelings spun and coalesced. Looking at her, he felt connected not only to his past but also to his future, as if he were standing at a crossroads in his life and seeing all the possibilities of his actions played out for him, here and now.

He had to make a tremendous decision. One he knew would determine which road he went down. "I've got to ask because I need to know—why did you kick me out back at the cabin, say those awful things to me?"

"I'm sorry." Her eyes teared up again. "I didn't want to hurt you, but I didn't want you getting hurt either. I'm toxic, radioactive, and I don't want you to die because you're standing too close to me."

He cupped her cheek, and she pressed her face against his palm. "I understand the trouble you're in and I'm choosing to stand with you. All you have to do is let me."

"But the thought of anything happening to you," she said, shaking her head as tears fell. "It just guts me. Then there's Olivia. Sometimes I think that I should send her to live with my parents. Give her the stability she needs. They'd love her, hug her every day, watch over her, make sure that she has a cake on her birthday."

"I can't tell you what to do, but I know you'd miss her. And what happens once you do clear your name? Will they just give her back?"

"No. They'd fight me in court. I know it. But what if I *don't* clear my name?"

"What if Ryker found out that Olivia was with your parents? There'd be nothing to stop him from snatching her. Your parents won't be able to keep her safe from him."

Shutting her eyes, she trembled against him.

"Do you really want to know what I think?" he asked.

She looked up at him and caressed his cheek. "Yes."

"We question Bertrand. See what he knows. Get everything you can from him. Then you'll need to contact Hunter. Remember, the Warriors didn't do it alone."

She twined her arms around his neck and hugged him.

"I also think you should take Olivia." He pressed his cheek to hers.

"John," she whispered, the word trembling as her body did the same, the shiver running through him, as well. "I'm afraid for Olivia and for you."

But not for herself. Did she have any idea how amazing she was?

He pulled back, needing to see her. When their eyes met, his decision was made. No doubt. No stupefaction. "I love you, Zee. Your fight is my fight, and I haven't lost one yet. I can help you keep Olivia safe. As long as we're together, I don't want you to be afraid."

She put her forehead to his and sobbed quietly. "You love me?" she asked as if it couldn't possibly be true, but underlying her disbelief, he heard fear.

"I do. I love you." He cradled her head and stroked her hair. "Don't. Please don't cry, sweetheart." There was nothing quite so astonishing and terrifying to him as this strong woman with a backbone of steel in tears.

"You could have your pick of women if you wanted." She sobbed. "It would be so much easier for you with someone else. Have a nice quiet life."

He'd tried nice and quiet in Alaska for three years

and hated every second of it until he'd found her. "I don't want easy. I don't need safe. I want complicated." The more difficult and complex, the better. Hell, give him impossible, if it meant that his life still had purpose. "I need you."

They were perfect for each other, if only she could see it. Feel the certainty that was like a fist in his gut telling him that they were meant to be.

"I wish you didn't love me." She drew in a shuddering breath. "You tell me not to be afraid, but I'm worried that I'll get you ki—"

He drew her to him and kissed the word from her lips, swallowing the bad luck without letting her put it in the air. But the electricity of that instant connection was exhilarating, like jumping off a cliff. Like being in free fall before you hit the ground.

"John." She eased back.

He wondered if he had messed up completely. Misread her, misread everything. Wanting his help and wanting him might not be one and the same.

"I love you," she whispered, her breath fanning his lips. "And I've wanted you so much, for so long that I dream about you sometimes."

A riot of emotions exploded in his chest from relief to rapture. It was as if he'd won the lottery.

Instead of taxes, he'd have to deal with Ryker and Delta team, but as long as Zee loved him in return, he was a winner.

"Tell me about your dreams." He hoped they were sweet and sexy. Naughty but all good.

"I'd rather show you." She leaned in and brushed her mouth over his.

His blood caught on fire, and he kissed her. It wasn't soft or exploratory. No, this was about total possession. The mutual kind, where they claimed each other.

She lay back on the bed, bringing him down with her, settling his hips between her spread legs. Her tongue curling against his and the unreserved sensuality in the way she'd sucked on it, the press of her body to his, eager and responsive, lured him in, driving him wild like no other. Knocked him so crazy that the need to be inside her was like the beat of a drum pounding through him.

Cupping her buttocks, he lifted her hips, drawing her closer so that his erection was nestled in the soft notch of her legs. He rubbed her back and forth against him, groaning aloud at the exquisite pressure.

He ran a hand down the swell of her breast, stroking the hourglass of her curves, lower, playing over her hip bone. Lower still into her pants, between her thighs, and he slipped one finger, then two inside her, and she gasped.

All he could do was revel in the slick softness between her legs and feel the wet heat of her. "I can't believe how ready you are for me." He pressed his thumb to that sensitive bundle of nerves and her body arched and trembled while her lips clung to his and she caressed every inch of him as she rocked against his hand.

The last time he'd wanted a woman so much had been…never. Not even as a teenager with raging hormones. His desire for her went deeper than the physical. Zee was everything that he had been waiting for and needed in his life.

But he didn't want her to make an impulsive decision. He wanted to be the love of her life. Not a one-hit wonder that she'd regret.

Because once they were together, one time wouldn't be enough for him. He'd need days. Weeks. Years with her. He was completely hooked.

"Are you sure?" he asked, giving her a chance to reconsider. "I don't have protection." The need to make that as clear as his desire was important. Doubly so after what she'd been through with that psycho. "I got a clean bill of health from the service and haven't been with anyone since, but if you want me to stop, I will."

She took his face in both her hands and held his gaze. "I'm one hundred percent certain, and healthy and covered on birth control." She kissed him. Then she pulled off both layers of tops over his head and started to undo his belt. "I want you, John. Right. Now."

He'd never heard sweeter words.

DESIRE RUSHED THROUGH HER like a high-speed train as John peeled her clothes from her body and kissed her all over.

It had been three years since she'd been on a date, and that had ended after one cup of coffee and a handshake. Kisses and sex had been reserved for her fantasies. Ryker had been the last man she'd been with. Perhaps that was odd, made her weird, but she could never get comfortable with anyone. Always felt watched. Stalked, even though Ryker hadn't been around. There was also the fear that a potential boyfriend might one day turn into another monster.

The hassle and the risk weren't worth it. Not with Olivia to think of. Zee had never even noticed her lack of a sex life or wished to change that until John.

Running her hands over the patchwork of scars on his torso, she knew the healed pucker marks of bullet wounds, the severe lines of old knife cuts. There were other blemishes, too, that she couldn't begin to guess at. His body was a map of violence survived, and it made her want to love him even more.

Her body cradled his now, instinctively welcoming him. She let out a greedy sound, not even thinking they might be getting too deep, too fast. There was only need. Hunger for this man that she was tired of denying.

As his fingers slid into her again, he held her wrists above her head with his other hand. Stared down at her face and watched every feeling she couldn't hide with such raw intensity that it brought her closer to the brink. She moved her mouth up to taste him, but he kept his lips just out of reach, his fingers stroking, teasing…sensual torture that made her writhe beneath him and had her begging him not to stop.

It wasn't enough. Not even close. But she was seconds from reaching that sweet peak. Shudders overtook her and she cried out.

His head dipped then, swiftly catching her mouth and swallowing her cries of pleasure. His tongue slicked over hers in total possession. He made a guttural sound in his throat, kissing her deeper.

She hadn't known it could be like this. That kissing could be intoxicating. Addictive.

"You're so beautiful," he rasped, his deep voice rippling through her. "But when you climax, you're drop-dead gorgeous."

John kissed a path down her body, featherlight, and crouched between her thighs, using his big shoulders to push her legs wider apart. Then his mouth latched on to her and she bucked at the intense sensations that bombarded her from his lips and the deep swipe of his tongue. Waves of pleasure rolled through her body.

No man had gone down on her since college. Ryker hadn't been interested in giving, only receiving and taking.

Grabbing the back of John's head, she urged him closer. The pressure built inside her, twisting deeper than before. Her toes curled. Her legs locked, muscle shaking. Everything in her tightened and squeezed, pleasure centering where his mouth was on her, his tongue laving, bringing her so much ecstasy it verged on agony. She moaned, screamed, coming apart in a loud, embarrassing way, and she was grateful the house was empty.

In a heartbeat, he was poised over her, forearms braced down on the bed on either side of her head. A corner of his mouth kicked up in a self-satisfied grin right before he was drinking the last sounds of her release from her lips.

She needed him inside her. After unzipping his

pants, she helped him get them off. Along the way, she appreciated the landscape of his body. Taut, muscular chest. Sculpted arms. Ridged abdomen. A thin happy trail that led to his arousal.

Her inner muscles clenched at a stab of apprehension.

"It's been a long time for me." Eleven years. "And you're…" She glanced down at him. *Too big.* "Well-endowed."

He palmed between her thighs and she arched up from the bed. "I'll go slow, but trust me, I belong here."

Shifting their bodies, he changed position so quickly and with such remarkable strength, putting her on top. Giving her full control of everything. She settled on top of him, straddling his hips. Taking him in her hand and guiding him where they both wanted him to be, she lowered herself slowly down on him.

They both gasped as he entered her.

He growled, "You're tight." Clutching her hips, he threw back his head against the bed. "You feel so good."

Everything melted and softened inside her at knowing she brought him pleasure.

She rocked her pelvis, bringing him deeper. They found an easy, steady rhythm. Feeling sexy and empowered, utterly alive, she bucked her hips, loving the fact that finally she was with John.

Suddenly, he rolled, flipping their bodies, bringing her beneath him. "Is this okay?" he rasped.

She smiled. "Better than okay."

He went slowly as he promised, but from the

strained look on his face she could only imagine how much self-control it took on his part. Running her hands over his body, she kissed him and encouraged him with her touch to go deeper, faster, harder, if he wanted. Her inner muscles loosened, stretching for him and she trusted him not to hurt her.

This was what lovemaking should be. Connection. Trust. Not holding anything back.

The brush of his mouth sent waves of sensation vibrating along every nerve ending. She clutched his shoulders, her fingers curling into the lean muscles of his body. The texture and taste of his mouth, his hot tongue as necessary as air as it stroked against hers. The feel of all that muscle pressing down on her with him buried deep inside was completely devastating.

Her body ached and hummed. He felt so good it was frightening. She never wanted this to end. He was close, his body tensing, going faster, powering deep and providing friction in all that right places that surprisingly brought her to the edge again, too.

With one last deep thrust, he grunted through his release, holding her tight, and she followed, spiraling to the other side along with him.

She'd read articles about how women could be multiorgasmic but had never believed it before. Not until him.

Panting, chest heaving, he pulled her close so that she lay snuggled against his side with her hand on his chest, her thigh on his. He put his palm on hers and threaded their fingers.

This was real. John was in her arms. He'd listened to all her secrets without judgment and had chosen to stand by her, to love her. She hugged him tighter, languid. Happy and hopeful.

"One minute." He shifted up and away, slipping out of the bed.

She heard the tap go on in the bathroom. A few seconds later he returned, the bed depressing as he sat. He trailed a hand across her hip, down her thigh and hitched her leg. Gently, he cleaned between her thighs with a warm washcloth.

The intimate gesture was so unbelievably sweet and thoughtful, it made her chest ache with love.

"We should leave soon, for Idaho Falls," he said.

"Can I get two more minutes with you first?" It had been so long since she'd been held. She missed the simple act of cuddling. "I like the feel of your arms around me."

He leaned back against the headboard, resettling her between his legs and tugging her into the cradle of his arms to rest against him. She put her cheek to his chest, curling an arm around his waist while he wrapped her in a warm embrace.

"I can do better than two. How about ten." He scooped her hair away and pressed his mouth to the side of her neck. "When we get back, I'll hold you all night."

"You might not have much choice in this tiny bed."

He chuckled and the deep rumble vibrated through her, soothing her in a way she hadn't expected. She'd never felt more at peace, oddly enough.

It made her wonder if they were in the eye of the storm. But one never knew when the eye would pass and then the scariest, nastiest, gnarliest part would follow.

She clung tighter to John.

"There's something I never told you," he said in a low voice, stroking her arm.

"What's that?"

"The day you knocked on my door, introduced yourself to borrow a cup of sugar and sidled up to me—"

"I did *not* sidle up to you."

Another deep chuckle from him—a sound she adored so much. "Yeah, you did, and I didn't mind one bit."

She preferred to think of it as facilitating friendship with a pie. After he'd opened his door and she'd seen *him*, touched him, that's when she'd decided to ask for the cup of sugar. He never even knew she had to use the entire cup for the one pie that she had baked for him.

"Was it my stunning good looks or charming personality?" he asked.

"I'll admit you're very easy on the eyes." She ran her nose up his neck and kissed along his jaw. "And your personality is not only charming but also compelling. But I immediately felt comfortable around you. Safe. I never worried that you'd drug my food and do something untoward to me."

She'd also been intrigued by him and attracted to him. Drawn. Something about his intense green eyes and that palpable aura of power and strength that pulled her to him, like an iron to lodestone.

Not that she had a predilection for big strong men

who could easily overpower her. When it came to guys, she hadn't known what cup of tea she'd enjoy, only that she'd been thirsty for a long time.

He stroked her hair. "What I never told you was that after we met and I saw how gorgeous you were, I was worried for you. So I made my rounds to the guys in the area that I knew and told them that you had moved in."

"I was trying to keep a low profile and you told people about me?" She hit his leg playfully.

"Have you looked in the mirror? You can't keep a low profile even in the wilderness. Trust me, they would've noticed you on their own. I told them that you were my new neighbor *in shouting distance* of me," he said, and she glanced up at him, "and that if anyone messed with you, they messed with me." He gave her one of those smiles, and her heart moved in her chest.

No wonder he'd insisted that she have the two-way radio handy when they weren't together. That was the reason she'd kept it on the nightstand while she slept. "You did that for me? Even though we weren't dating?"

"Sure. Like I said, I was worried. It made me feel better that you carried a gun everywhere and had those perimeter alarms."

Leave it to a former Navy SEAL to notice everything.

"Don't get me wrong," he continued, "I secretly hoped you were interested in more than playing chess with me and swapping goods, but that's not why I was looking out for you. It was just the right thing to do."

There were a lot of jerks in the world and a few psychos like Ryker, but thank goodness there were men of integrity such as John. He truly was the best.

John held her a little longer, their ten minutes flying by, feeling like two, but it was best for them to get a move on. He left a note for Mike and Enola, explaining they had an important errand to run, that they'd return late, and jotted down the number to Zee's burner phone in case of an emergency. Before she knew it, they were in the car and on the road.

"What's the plan?" he asked.

"Luisa's father is a minister, and he has a church in Idaho Falls. I'm sure they'll have a Christmas Eve service. We should start there."

Chapter Sixteen

John drove through Idaho Falls, getting his bearings in the city while they found the church. The house of worship's parking lot was full and the streets adjacent to the building were lined with cars, indicating a packed house for the Christmas Eve service. Two streets down from the church, he found a spot to park in front of Cup of Joe.

Zee thought the local coffee shop or public library would offer the best chance for her to use free Wi-Fi in the vicinity of the building. But they didn't have a direct line of sight on the church from the library.

Here they could keep an eye out for Luisa while allowing Zee to hack into the CIA's database one last time and download the information her malware collated.

Her fingers flew across the keyboard as she sat in the passenger seat working on her spare laptop from the duffel bag. "I'm in," she said.

That meant the clock was officially ticking on how long they could stay in Idaho Falls before Delta or some other team showed up. He didn't know how much time they had, but he figured at least two to three hours. Delta team was already mobilized but they didn't know where Zee was. Once they found out, it would take them time to travel. With any luck, they were in Seattle trying to figure out their next step.

John climbed out of the car and went into Cup of Joe. Every chunky armchair was occupied, and holiday music flowed from the speakers.

He ordered a black coffee for Zee and a cappuccino for himself. "Hey, do you have any idea how long the Christmas Eve service at the church lasts?" he asked the barista.

"Less than an hour. We expect to have a full house in here in about twenty minutes. Folks always stop in after the service."

"Thanks." He sipped the cappuccino and moaned with the delight.

Stopping by the car, he set Zee's coffee in the cup holder for her since she was typing away furiously on the laptop and then he crossed the street to hit a store that had caught his eye. The bell at the top of the door rang as he entered the toy store.

They had things arranged in age-appropriate groups. It took him a couple of minutes to decide on Dungeons & Dragons Adventure Begins and a pink instant camera for Olivia. In the age of cell phones and selfies, the kid probably didn't know what a Polaroid was. He took the items to the register. One gift for her birthday. One for Christmas. He didn't think it was fair to deny her an extra present because they fell on the same day.

From the front of the store, he could see the

church. The doors were closed, and the street was quiet. He used his debit card since the CIA would know that they were there within minutes if they didn't already.

Service was still ongoing two blocks down, so he made one more stop at a bath shop. An explosion of fragrances bombarded him as he crossed the threshold. Since Zee enjoyed a good, long soak in a tub, he headed for the bath oils. Not that she'd get to use it anytime soon, but she would appreciate the gesture. A tropical scented oil reminded him of her. She always smelled like a luscious mix of coconut and flowers. *Everywhere.* From her hair to between her thighs.

The sooner they found Luisa and hopefully David Bertrand the sooner he could get Zee back to Mike's attic, strip off her clothes and curl up in bed with her. The idea of making love to her again was more than a little appealing, but he'd be fine with holding her, too. He simply wanted to be close to her, as close as possible.

Never had he understood how his buddies could walk down the aisle and pledge to love one person for the rest of their days. Then again, Mike had done it three times. But John could see hitching himself to Zee. One woman. Forever.

Because she was the right one.

The thought was probably premature, but he'd keep it to himself.

As he crossed the street back to the car, the old injury in his leg ached something fierce. He hoped it meant they were in for a rainy Christmas, but he knew better.

Trouble was coming.

He dumped the bags in the back of the sedan as Zee pulled a thumb drive from the computer's port and powered off the laptop.

"It's done. I hope it was worth it." She glanced at the backseat. "What is all of that?"

"Christmas gift for you. Olivmas gifts for the kiddo."

"You're making me look bad."

"Impossible. You could never look bad. You're too beautiful." *Just as much on the inside as the outside.* He leaned over and kissed her, a quick, warm press of his lips against hers.

"Your gift is in ashes. It was back in my cabin."

"What was it?"

"A backgammon set with a leather case."

That would've been perfect. "It's the thought that counts."

She rubbed his thigh and he smiled at the way she touched him. Intimate. Possessive.

He finished his cappuccino and then checked the ammo on the gun with the attached sound suppressor that he'd lifted from one of the Delta team guys at the academy. Almost a full clip, two bullets missing. He had pumped the slugs into a member of their team.

Zee had her gun and baton, both holstered.

They didn't expect any problems from Luisa Morales or David Bertrand in the event they found him, but preparation for the unknown never hurt anyone.

"What do Morales and Bertrand look like?" John asked.

"Luisa is thin, delicate-looking. Light-colored hair. Big brown eyes. Full lips. In every picture or shot of her on CCTV, she's in full makeup with a bold lip color. That's the way I remember her. Always fashionable. David has salt-and-pepper hair, he's on the trim side, fair complexion, average height. Maybe five-ten. Nothing distinctive about him beside a little limp like one leg is shorter than the other."

"Have you ever seen her with a guy here in Idaho Falls?"

"I've only observed her for a limited time, and she was always on her own or with her parents, I think. But it's the holidays. People get sentimental. Sloppy."

John couldn't help but think of him and Zee. They had gotten sentimental, going so far as to confess their true feelings and make love for the first time— something he'd replayed in his head during the three-hour drive, but hopefully they hadn't been sloppy in a way that would come back to bite them.

Finally, the church doors opened. The congregation poured out onto the sidewalk. People were holding lit white candles, chatting and giving hugs goodbye.

Zee perked up in her seat, putting the coffee down in a cup holder.

"Do you see her?" John asked.

Staring through the windshield, Zee scanned the crowd. John started the car and repositioned closer, parking in front of a fire hydrant.

It wasn't until the crowd thinned and most of the

congregation had traipsed off that Zee said, "There she is. Light gray coat with a furry collar."

The woman stood out in a crowd. Her hair was pulled back in a tight bun and she wore an elegant wool pillbox hat that matched her coat. She had her arm linked with a man's. He was dressed in a dark suit. Dark wool overcoat. Mousy-brown hair.

"He doesn't match Bertrand's description." When Zee didn't respond, he said, "Maybe she moved on. Found someone else out here."

"Maybe. But I remember this one time, after a particularly difficult mission that David had been a part of, Hunter had a barbecue at his town house. David had brought Luisa. She was all over him and not in some contrived, fake way. It was a genuine handsy-feely thing where she was calling him *pookie* all night, ad nauseam, and David had looked like he'd crawl over broken glass for her. Do absolutely anything to keep that woman. Perhaps he'd be willing to gain weight and dye his hair, too."

John understood that feeling all too well. He was willing to do anything to be with Zee, to help her keep Olivia safe, especially from a maniac like Ryker.

Zee pulled her hair up into a ponytail and twirled it into a bun, securing it with an elastic band. Tugging on a cable-knit wool hat, she covered her head and slipped on black gloves. "I'm going to get a closer look. If they hop in a car, follow slowly and I'll get back in."

He put a hand on her forearm, stopping her. "Let me hoof it. You get behind the wheel."

"John, I used to do this as my job for the CIA. I didn't always sit behind a computer. They trained me well. Hunter chose me because as a woman, I can blend in where men can't. Or because he knew that a man would look at me and see a pretty face instead of a deadly weapon. No one will perceive me as a threat. I'll be fine." She jumped out of the car.

No one but Bertrand, he would've told her if she'd given him the chance.

She was forgetting that the analyst knew precisely what she was capable of. If the man with Luisa was indeed Bertrand in disguise and he got a glimpse of Zee, he would be gone faster than spit in the wind, and then they would be back at square one.

Gritting his teeth, John kept the engine running and watched.

Zee hurried down the sidewalk, crossed the street and disappeared in the throng of the congregation.

Luisa hugged the minister and the woman beside him, presumably her mother. With air kisses and one last wave, she took the arm of the man next to her and the two proceeded down the street.

The man in the dark suit strode with a slight yet distinctive limp. A positive sign, but not definitive confirmation as he had hoped. The couple passed the church's parking lot and continued strolling.

They were either parked farther away or in walking distance of their destination.

Zee wasn't far behind them, but she wasn't close enough to be easily spotted either. Head down, she moved like a shadow, gently winding past others in a manner that made the gaggle of evening parishioners seem oblivious.

John threw the car in Drive, pulled out from the space and rolled down the road.

Three blocks down, Zee crossed the street in front of the car. He stopped and let her in.

"I think they might be going home," she said. "The church owns a large plot of land not far from here. They recently started a rent-to-own program for mobile homes to bring in income."

"They run a trailer park," he said.

"Apparently. Luisa is renting to own. She has been since she relocated here."

"The boyfriend lives with her?" he asked.

Zee shrugged. "I don't know. This is the first I've seen of him."

"What do you think of the limp? It's not quite what you described."

As they crept down the street in the car, Zee's gaze was glued to the couple.

"If that is Bertrand," she said, "the limp has changed. Improved."

Which wasn't possible. But what were the odds of her dating two men in a row with limps?

Not high.

"Maybe he's wearing a lift in his shoe to compensate for the limp," she said. "To lessen it. Hide it."

That was an explanation John could buy into. "Yeah, maybe."

The couple turned left into the mobile home park. There weren't any other vehicles parked alongside the road in front of the community and he didn't want their sedan to stand out.

"Do you know which trailer she lives in?" he asked.

"I know the number, 221. But not exactly where it's located in there."

John threw the car in Reverse and parked on the rear side of the mobile park in the shadow of a Dumpster and some trees as a precaution. They got out of the car and darted across the street to the brick wall that enclosed the park.

"Give me your foot. I'll boost you." He cupped his hands, forming a stirrup.

She shoved her foot into the supportive grip. He hoisted her up, and she caught hold of the top of the six-foot wall and lifted herself over. John hopped up easily and climbed over, but he was careful to land with most of his weight on his good leg.

They skirted around a couple of trash bins and hurried along the center path through the park, which was paved. She searched the numbers on the sides of the homes while he stayed sharp and on the lookout for any nosy neighbors who might spot them.

Zee took a sharp turn to the right, leading him deeper into the community. Ducking down near a trailer, she waved at him to take a knee and pointed. "That one is Luisa's."

There were two windows on the front side. He guessed the living area in the middle and the bedroom at the far left.

The lights were on in the center of the trailer, the living room.

"How do you want to play this?" he asked Zee.

"I knock on the door and see what happens."

A bold proposition that might give better results than snooping through the window or breaking in. Either way they needed to talk to the couple inside.

"Okay," he said, glancing around. "I've got your back."

He drew his weapon. Not knowing what they were walking into, he figured it best to be prepared and have no need to use the gun than be unprepared and filled with regrets.

Staying crouched low, they moved forward to the trailer marked 221.

As Zee climbed the front steps, he noticed a flurry of movement inside through the window. She knocked, and they both waited.

The door swung open inward, and Zee pushed her way inside the trailer without waiting for an invitation or wasting valuable time trying to convince the woman to let them in.

Luisa gasped and stumbled back, disappearing in the trailer.

John scanned the surrounding area before crossing the threshold to make sure no one snuck up behind them. A force of habit he couldn't break. He closed the door and locked it.

"Oh, my God!" Luisa's palms were raised in the air like this was a stickup.

The man in the suit stood in the kitchen holding a shotgun.

Zee lifted her hands, showing that they were

empty, but John trained his weapon on the man with the twelve-gauge in his hands.

"I know you," Luisa said, recognition dawning on her face.

Zee nodded. "We met once at a barbecue in Virginia. You were with David."

"Yeah, I remember," Luisa said. "Baby?" She turned and looked over her shoulder back at the man.

"David?" Zee inched forward. "Is that you?"

"Zenobia." The man tilted his head to the side, staring at her. "What are you doing here?"

"Just to talk," she said. "To ask you a few questions. Then we'll leave. I promise," she said, waving at John to put his weapon down.

But he wasn't going to lower the gun until the other man did.

David's gaze bounced between them. His shoulders relaxed, and he plopped down in a chair at the table in the kitchen, setting the shotgun on the wooden surface.

The room buzzed with tension. John stayed on high alert, keeping his gun close to his chest but lowering the muzzle.

"How did you find me?" David asked.

"I didn't. I found Luisa. Figured you two might be together."

David lowered his head and sighed.

"I'm sorry." Luisa went to his side. "I should've done a better job of covering my tracks."

"I learned that you were fired after what happened," Zee said. "I came to see what you might know. We need your help."

His gaze shifted to John. "Who is he?"

"A friend," she said, but this time the word didn't burn his gut. "Someone I trust with my life. He's one of the good guys—I assure you."

"I'm not sure there are any good guys anymore." David ripped off his drab brown wig, revealing salt-and-pepper hair. He took off his suit jacket, unbuttoned his shirt and removed the top piece of a fat suit. "I'm not as savvy and creative as you guys, able to transform into a different person like something from *Mission Impossible*, but I was flying under the radar and undiscovered until you came here. What do you want?"

"You were fired," Zee said. "Right after our last mission." She stepped deeper into the trailer, crossing in front of the one of the windows.

John grabbed her arm and pulled her back. He hated these flimsy trailers. The lightness that made mobile homes easily transportable also meant they weren't as sturdy as a standard house. He felt vulnerable pinned in place inside this tin can. Every window was a point of further exposure.

He sure as hell wasn't going to let either of them stand in front of windows, announcing their presence.

Faces couldn't be seen from the drawn sheer curtains, but anyone watching would be able to tell that someone was standing there. If more than two people were seen moving around inside, it might signal a change of pattern, that something was off.

"What did you find that made you disappear and go underground?" Zee asked.

"I don't want any trouble." David gave a grave shake of his head, his gaze hardening. "I just want to live my life, marry Luisa, have a couple of kids."

A sad smile tugged at Luisa's lips. "Oh, pookie."

"None of us want trouble." Zee sighed at him. "My daughter, Olivia, turns eleven tomorrow. All I want is peace and quiet, but I can't give her a safe, stable home unless I can figure out what went wrong on my team's last mission. I think you know what it is. Please, I'm begging you. Tell me."

"I've stayed safe this long," David said, standing up and walking closer, "because I've kept my mouth shut and haven't caused any trouble. The minute I start talking to you, all that changes. I may as well flush my life here down the toilet. It might be selfish, but I'm not ready to do that."

"You're already talking to her," John said, holding tight to Zee's arm. "And they know it." Or they would soon enough. That's how the CIA worked. "Her kid was almost taken yesterday. She could've been killed. They both could've been."

"Taken?" David's hands trembled. "Wait, there's a team tracking you and you came here? What in the hell is wrong with you?"

"They know Luisa is here," Zee said. "This location is blown for you. That's the other reason we're here, to warn you. A team will eventually show up on your doorstep. You need to leave tonight."

"What?" Luisa said.

"Go pack our things," David told her.

"But what about Mom and Dad? We can't leave them behind."

"We'll discuss it in the car after we're packed."

Luisa nodded and ran to the bedroom. David opened a cabinet in the kitchen and pulled out a coffee canister. He flipped off the lid, grabbed a roll of money and shoved it into his pocket.

"Please, help me, David," Zee said. "Help all of us. Hunter. Dean. Gage. Olivia. My team was set up and I think you know it."

David rubbed a hand across his forehead, down over his face, and grabbed hold of his chin. "I did find something."

"No, don't say anything," Luisa said from the bedroom. "We talked about this. You're not obligated to endanger yourself any further. You did what you could, you tried, but you don't owe them anything."

"What did you try to do?" Zee asked, but he didn't respond. "You'll have to keep running just like us until we clear our names."

David walked out of the kitchen and strode into the living room. "I found discrepancies in the mission, after it was all said and done."

"What kind of discrepancies?" John asked.

"The description of Khayr Faraj's birthmark for one. Turns out that it's shaped like a tree on his left cheek. But in the file, it was—"

"Shaped like an apple on his right cheek," Zee said, cutting him off.

David nodded. "Someone changed it. Other things were different, too. When the mission was first input into the system, it had the usual parameters, where the team decides how to execute the objective. But it had been altered later to specify the target should be eliminated in a bombing."

"Was there anything else that you can remember?" Zee asked. "Any other discrepancies?"

This was taking too long. John didn't like lingering someplace that wasn't safe, but the one thing in their favor was they had a healthy lead on Delta team. They should be able to put plenty of miles between themselves and this trailer by the time danger came a calling.

"No," David said, mouth thinned, "but that was enough to lead me to believe that they never wanted you to kill Faraj in the first place. I think the Afghan official Ashref Saleh was the intended target all along."

"The Afghans are our allies," John said.

"He would never be considered a sanctioned target," Zee said, shaking her head. "Only as collateral damage after he handed over the money to Faraj proving his complicity."

"Yet, he never handed over any money to Faraj because Faraj wasn't at the meeting and your team still ended up killing Saleh anyway."

John's throat went dry. "Because someone wanted her team to believe that the tribal leader with a slightly different birthmark was Faraj."

"I think so. It'd looked to me like you were set up." David walked around the small living room as he spoke. "I couldn't find any evidence that the Afghan official was corrupt or funding terrorism. I have no idea where those mission details came from, other than from someone's imagination. That someone wanted Ashref Saleh dead and used Team Topaz to do it."

She stepped forward and John hauled her back again. They needed to wrap this up and get out of there.

"But who would do it?" Zee asked.

David shrugged. "I don't know who is responsible."

Zee exhaled a shaky breath. "What about the proof of the discrepancies? Do you have copies?"

"Copies? Are you kidding me?" David asked. "If I had copies, I'm sure I would've been killed instead of fired."

"Who fired you?" John wondered. "Did you show anyone what you found?"

"Someone must have been monitoring my online activity. I started digging around—shortly thereafter, I was locked out of the system and escorted out of the building by security with no explanation. I had a bad feeling. Knew better than to make waves about it and disappeared."

"I don't understand why anyone would believe that we killed Ashref Saleh for no reason without giving us a chance to explain ourselves?"

"Everyone believed it because of the money," David said.

Zee grimaced. "What money?"

Luisa hurried to David's side, carrying a suitcase, and putting a comforting arm around his shoulder. "You've said too much already. We agreed to stay out of this. To protect ourselves."

"She found me." David's manner shifted. "She's

asking. She needs to know. They all do." David looked at Zee. "There are four offshore accounts in the Cayman Islands. One in each of your names with balances of 500,000 dollars."

Holy hell. John whistled. *Two million dollars.*

Staring at David with her face contorted in shock, Zee said unsteadily, "What? But we were never paid off."

David frowned at her. "Try telling that to the Agency and anyone who will listen. That's why the kill order was approved without an investigation."

"But we never took any money." Zee's voice grew agitated. "It must still be sitting there."

"That doesn't prove you weren't paid off," David said. "Only that you didn't get a chance to enjoy the money because the CIA found out about it before you could and froze the accounts."

Zee cradled her head in her hands, her mouth gaped in disbelief.

Red beams of laser sights slashed into the room, painting spots on David and Luisa. A chill rushed down John's spine like the icy fingers of a wraith. He yelled for the couple to duck, but he was slow. *Too slow.*

Gunfire shattered the windows, pumping lead into David and Luisa.

John lunged, bringing Zee down to the floor. She covered her head, her body jumping in reaction to the startling barrage of bullets. A cold sweat broke out on his neck.

Luisa and David were both dead. There was nothing that could be done for them now.

His gaze darted around the trailer in search of some means of escape. John had to get Zee out of there before Delta stormed in.

Chapter Seventeen

They were dead. Because of her.

Zee stared at Luisa and David, regretting that she came there. But how did Delta vector in on this location so quickly?

They couldn't have already been in Idaho unless...

Her laptop. She'd left traces of her deep dive into Luisa on the hard drive. Led them straight here.

"Listen to me," John said in her ear over the gunfire. "We have to get out of here."

"How?"

"I have an idea. We need to crawl to the kitchen. Find anything combustible and put it in the microwave."

"What?" He wanted to create a bomb?

"Trust me. Move."

They crawled through the trailer as Delta team riddled the mobile home with bullets.

In the kitchen, Zee grabbed two cans of nonstick cooking spray and any aerosol cleaning supplies from under the kitchen sink that she could find.

John snatched the shotgun from the table and began pumping holes into the laminate floor.

She threw the aerosol sprays into the microwave.

Put under enough pressure and heated to the point that they'd burst would turn the canisters into a weapon.

"Set it for five minutes."

Doing as he told her, she turned the microwave on, essentially activating a powerful improvised explosive device.

He kicked at the holes he made in the floor with the shotgun, enlarging them. The thin laminate and layer of plywood beneath gave way easily under his boot heel until the hole was large enough for them fit through.

The metal inside the microwave sparked and crackled within seconds. That thing was going to explode in less than five minutes.

He got her down through the opening first and quickly followed.

They scrambled through the underbelly beneath the home. The gunfire died down, stopping altogether, but they quickened their pace.

The homemade bomb was going to blow and when it did, they needed to be clear of the blast.

John kicked out the lattice board that skirted the bottom of the home. The noise be damned. They had to move. She shimmied through the hole and he was right behind her.

They took off running toward the rear of the trailer park as the windows on the mobile home shattered, sending a hail of glass and shrapnel toward the parking lot.

Gunshots rang out behind them.

They both sprinted for the brick wall at the back

of the community, weaving around trailers to prevent anyone from a getting a direct shot at them.

At the wall, she climbed on top of one of the trash bins to help her over. With a running start, John hopped up, grabbing the top of the wall and swung over to the other side. But when he touched the ground, a grunt escaped his mouth and he limped forward.

He must've landed wrong.

"Go to the car," she said. "Get it started. I'll cover you."

Men were going to be hot on their tails and John's injury was going to slow them down. This made the most sense.

He clenched his jaw, either in pain or protest or both. But there was no time to argue.

She took aim at the top of the wall. Sure enough, the head of a Delta operative popped up as the man began climbing. She squeezed the trigger, sending him back over from where he came.

John took off, made it to the car. The engine cranked down the street. Tires screeched forward and the vehicle stopped behind her. "Come on. Get in."

Zee spun around, lowering her weapon. John had opened the back door for her.

As she dove inside, a hot spike of fire tore through her flesh.

RYKER STOOD ON the roof of a trailer that was adjacent to the rear wall. Squeezing the trigger, he fired two more bullets as the silver sedan squealed down the street and careened around the corner.

Damn. He hadn't even gotten the license plate.

He might not have stopped them and couldn't track the car, but he had shot Zee. Of that he was certain. It wasn't fatal. She didn't deserve a quick death and his daughter wasn't in the car.

Ryker needed to find Olivia before he killed that woman.

They had stashed his daughter somewhere.

But Zee would never leave Olivia alone. Especially not in a motel. The child would be with someone Zee trusted. Not that she knew anyone in this part of the country.

His thoughts churned. Maybe she had enough faith in her lover to leave Olivia with someone that Lowry trusted.

The door of the trailer he stood on opened. "Is someone up on my—"

Ryker aimed and pulled the trigger silencing the older man. Taking out his encrypted cell, he pushed the button, calling India on speed dial.

"Where you successful?" India asked.

"Bertrand has been eliminated. I'm still in pursuit of the main target. Compile a list of all of John Lowry's known associates. I need the names and addresses of any within a four-to-eight-hour drive of Idaho Falls. At the top of the list, I want to see those closest within the shortest drive of this location."

"Yes, sir. I'm on it."

LOOKING IN THE REARVIEW, John exhaled in relief. "I don't think we're being followed. It should be safe to hit the interstate."

Zee hissed in pain.

"What's wrong?" he asked.

"When it's possible, we need to pull over."

"Why?"

Zee's agonized gaze snapped up to the rearview mirror, and there was such pain in her face that it stole his breath. "I was hit."

His nerves wound tight as a metal spring. "How bad is it?"

She dug in her duffel, pulled out a cloth and pressed it to her left arm. "I'll live." Her voice was gritty as sandpaper. "The wound can wait until we're out of Idaho Falls. It's superficial," she said, but he doubted that she'd only been grazed.

It was best not to stop in the city. Better to get a few exits down on the interstate. His warrior goddess was putting logic ahead of medical care. He admired her strength more than she'd ever know.

John hit I-15 heading north and sped down the highway. Getting pulled over for exceeding the speed limit was a possibility, but he was willing to risk it. He spotted a sign for a rest stop ten miles away and pushed the accelerator past ninety until they'd reached it. If the car hadn't started rattling, he would've tried going even faster.

Parking far away from any other vehicles, he picked a well-lit spot under a lamppost. By the time he'd climbed into the backseat beside her, she'd slipped off her coat and had the tools that he needed from the medical kit waiting for him.

"You should've let me cover you instead." He cut up the sleeve of her top and peeled the fabric away from the wound. "You could've run to the car faster and we would've been out of there sooner."

"Hindsight is twenty-twenty. But that might have gone another way, too. If Ryker was the one who shot me," she said, looking down at her arm, "then he would've killed you. Not wounded you. Whereas he wants me to suffer before I die."

He cleaned her arm. "What are you saying, lucky you?"

She gave him a tight smile.

"There's an exit wound." No need to extract a bullet.

"See. Lucky."

If she weren't bleeding and in extreme pain—he was talking hell-on-fire kind of misery—he would've taken a second to kiss her.

They were both lucky. Unlike David and Luisa.

Instinct had kept John away from the windows and in turn kept Zee out of the line of fire in the trailer. He wished he could've saved David and Luisa, too. Ryker and that team of ruthless killers he was leading had no compunction about murdering innocent, unarmed people. They destroyed everything in their path, leaving a trail of carnage behind them.

One day, karma would come for them.

"When we get back to the house, maybe I should make the call to Hunter," she said. "Leave tonight."

"What about Olivmas? Maybe wait until tomorrow. Let her enjoy the day first. Cake. Presents. That sort of thing."

He tore open a package of Combat Gauze. The

dressing was pretreated with a powerful hemostatic agent and would stop arterial and venous bleeding in seconds. He put a piece on the entry and exit wounds and applied continuous pressure for a few minutes.

"Do you want to come with us?" she asked, not making eye contact when in his mind this topic had already been resolved. "I don't know where we'll be headed and if you'd prefer to stay, I'd understand. Just because we slept together and have feelings for each other doesn't mean there's a commitment here. I don't have any expectations."

For him, he was all in with big expectations, but the declaration felt a little profound, possibly too heavy-handed after what she'd said. "Wherever you two go, I want to go. If you'll have me."

"I'll take you, John." She caressed his face. "With pleasure. I just didn't want you to feel pressured. Obligated. I wanted you to have an out."

"Trust me—I don't want *out*." All. In.

Once the bleeding looked controlled, he wrapped her arm with fresh Combat Gauze and moved her to the front of the car.

He started the vehicle and drove to the interstate. "I don't know what I would've done if that bullet had hit a vital organ. I finally got you to admit how you feel about me. I can't lose you."

She put her hand on his leg and rubbed his thigh in that way he was starting to love. "Ditto, big guy."

Chapter Eighteen

"Michael Cutler," India said in Ryker's ear. "He's the only known associate within a thousand miles of Idaho Falls. Most of the people Lowry knows are in Coronado, California, or Virginia Beach. Cutler is originally from Montana and has a house there. The drive to Bertrand's could be down in less than three hours from his place."

"Their association?" Ryker asked.

"They've been close friends for twenty years. They went through BUD/S training together and served on the SEAL teams together. Numerous missions. Lowry acted as best man to Cutler three times."

He was the one. Zee would be at ease leaving Olivia with a SEAL as a protector. Ryker's daughter was at the Cutler residence.

"Give me an address and ETA," he said, referring to an estimated time of arrival. "Research the property. I need the best place to land and the most efficient way to cut the power before we breach the house."

"Regarding the power, sir, do you care if surrounding homes or the nearby town is affected?"

Was she for real?

"Do you know who I am?" Sometimes the analysts weren't aware of their true identities or their reputations.

"Yes, sir."

"Then you already have your answer."

Chapter Nineteen

The pain was excruciating, but Zee refused to complain or take anything for the discomfort beyond acetaminophen. She didn't want anything that would make her loopy.

With her coat draped over her shoulders, she trudged up the porch steps of Mike's house. John was beside her, carrying the duffel bag and his shopping bags. He was walking a little better, but she could tell that his leg was still bothering him.

The house was aglow with Christmas lights. Inside it looked as if most of the lights were on even though it was almost eleven.

Teenagers.

John opened the front door and they strolled inside. He locked it, put on the chain.

The oldest boys were on the sofa playing a shoot 'em up video game.

Mike and Enola were in the den dancing together in front of the fireplace.

"Hey," the boys said, both turning to look at them and their smiles fell.

Zee imagined how she must've looked to them. A

torn sleeve on her sweater. Gauze wrapped around her biceps. Bullet hole in the arm of coat. Blood stains.

"Are you okay?" the tallest boy asked, standing. Actually, he was a young man with a deep voice and looked strong enough to bench-press her weight with ease.

"Yeah, Tanner," John said. "She's fine. You guys go back to playing."

The alarm in Tanner's voice must have caught Mike's attention. Seconds later he was leaving Enola's side and coming into the living room. He looked her over and glanced at John.

"Why don't you go to the bedroom," John said to her. "I'll be up in a minute."

"Okay." She headed for the stairs as the two men spoke in hushed tones off to the side.

For a minute, she considered stopping by Amanda's room to check on Olivia and let her know that she was back, but after the reactions of the others to her appearance, she thought better of it.

She decided that she would wait until after midnight. The kids seemed as if they'd be up late and that way she could be the first to wish her daughter a happy birthday.

In the attic bedroom, she shrugged off her coat and sat.

John hurried up, shutting the door behind him. "It's all good," he said, answering her unspoken question. "Olivia had a great time at the winter carnival. I told Mike about the gunshot wound. A few details. He understood and told the boys not to say anything to Enola."

"I hate putting him in that position, where he's lying, omitting important things, to his wife."

"Mike is handling the situation the way he thinks is best and I happen to agree with him."

That told her a lot about John. Omission was okay in his book if he thought he was protecting someone he cared about.

He sat beside her. "Want any assistance getting out of those clothes?"

"Sure." She didn't need his help, but she wasn't opposed to accepting it.

They stripped, with him doing most of the work and then climbed into the bed beneath the covers. He switched on the radio that was on the nightstand. Soft instrumental music filled the room.

He pulled her into his arms and held her close. Dragged his knuckles across her hips. Let his fingers dance over legs and stomach. Cupped her breasts, feeling the weight of them in his palms. None of it was overtly sexual to make her think that this was foreplay, though she suspected he wouldn't turn her down if she suggested they make love. The way he touched her was tentative but intimate, like he was exploring new terrain that he'd laid claim to.

For a long time, they stayed that way, with him holding her, caressing her while she thought about all the little and big things that Mike hadn't shared with Enola. Things that John had thought it best to keep from her. Things Zee hadn't objected to because she'd been desperate for shelter.

"I need you to promise me something," she whispered.

"Anything. What is it?"

She sat up and looked at him. "Promise me that you'll never lie to me or omit sharing scary, dangerous things because you think it's best or that you're protecting me or whatever it is you guys tell yourselves. If we're together, then I need complete honesty."

His mouth hitched in a wry grin. "If you can promise the same in return, consider it done. But the second you break your word I'll go back to doing what I think is best."

"I can't believe you think I'll be the first to renege on this deal."

His smile deepened and she melted inside. "We'll see."

The music stopped.

Zee sat up and checked the radio, adjusting the volume and station. The clock face was dark.

Odd.

She glanced out the window behind the bed. The lights at the closest neighbor's house blinked out, followed by a wave of darkness spreading across the nearest town.

A firm, cold pressure ballooned in the bottom of her chest under her ribs. "John, something is wrong."

Turning toward the window, he looked at the sudden sea of darkness. "Get dressed."

They rushed around the room, throwing on their clothes and shoes. She slipped on her bulletproof vest before donning her sweater.

Zee peered out the window.

Men swarmed from the tree line, wearing NVGs and holding automatic weapons with red laser sights. They stalked across the property drawing closer to the house.

Her stomach bottomed out. "They're here."

Somehow Ryker had tracked them to the house. To this sanctuary filled with children.

Anger sliced her down the middle. She wanted Ryker's blood before he had a chance to hurt anyone else.

"Stay in the attic," John said. "Mike and I will handle this."

"There are children here," she snapped. Not only hers, but Mike and Enola's, as well.

"I know. We'll make sure nothing happens to them."

"I'm injured, but I'm not an *invalid*," she said, and the word had him stiffening. "Ryker wants me. They all do. I'm the target, the mission objective. I'll go out there, draw their attention by not using a silencer on my gun and lead them away. Ryker will follow. Some of the others will, too. Take out the rest who get into the house. Then come to the woods and help me. I'll run in that direction." She pointed out the window.

John's eyes drilled into her. "Hell, no! Over my dead body."

"We don't have time for this. That pack of cold-blooded killers is coming. And I'm not staying in this room."

He swore under his breath. Silence fell for a heartbeat, its presence suffocating. "I'm not going to talk you out of this, am I?" he asked.

"No. But no matter what happens, don't let Ryker get Olivia." She'd sacrifice her life for her daughter without a second thought.

"Mike has a rifle with a scope. I'm a good shot. Wait for me. I'll tell him what's happening, make sure the kids are hidden and get the rifle. Then you make a break for the woods. I'll pick off every bastard that chases you. Wait for me." John dashed for the door and hurried down the stairs.

Zee turned to the window.

Delta team was closing in. Any minute they would breach the house.

Dread pooled in her belly. The weight of it all pressed down on her. Not just the hours of running and fighting and battling to stay alive, but there was an ache in her soul. The consequence of all the choices she had made and the deaths she was responsible for. At the forefront of her mind were David and Luisa. They only wanted to stay safe, be happy, love one another.

No one else could die because of her. No one.

She had to do whatever was necessary to not only protect Olivia, but also the other children in the house, as well as John and Mike and Enola.

Unscrewing the sound suppressor, she took a deep breath. She tossed the silencer on the bed and pulled on her gloves.

She opened the window and looked around for a way to climb down.

To the side of the window ledge was a PVC pipe.

If the pain in her arm wasn't unbearable, she could make it without falling.

"THE STRIKE TEAM I told you about," John said, standing in the living room, "they're here."

Emotion flashed across Mike's face. Alarm. Rage. Resolve. "They came to the wrong house."

"They've got NVGs. Is your generator up and running?"

"Yeah," Mike said. "I'm tracking what you're thinking."

Light this place up bright enough for Santa to see from the North Pole and blind those fools, seizing the advantage.

"We've got to hide the kids somewhere safe," John said, "and I need Big Betty." That's what his buddy called his rifle with a scope.

"Mike, what's happening?" Enola asked, coming into the living room.

"No questions right now, babe," Mike said. "Round up the kids. Fast. Take everyone down to the cellar." He clapped his hands, and the sound sparked her into action.

Panic widened her eyes, but she ran up the stairs.

"Dad, what do you want us to do?" Tanner asked, standing beside his younger brother who was only a couple of inches shorter.

"Come on." Mike led the way to his office, flipping every light switch up along the way. He unlocked the gun case, pulled out a 9mm for himself, handed each of his sons a shotgun and tossed Big Betty to John. "Boys, help Enola with the kids."

Mike threaded a sound suppressor to the barrel of his weapon. "Anyone other than us comes into the cellar, blow them away."

"Yes, sir." The boys took off, leaving the room.

John snatched a box of ammo and dashed out of the office while Mike ran for the back door where the generator was in the yard.

Enola shepherded the frightened kids down to the first floor, shushing them not to ask questions, and led them around the corner to the cellar door.

Olivia cast a glance at John, her face stoic as she hurried with the others.

"It'll be all right," he said to her. Whatever it took, he'd make sure of it.

Tanner and his brother were close behind the kids and shut the cellar door once they were all inside.

On his way back up the stairs, John loaded Big Betty.

Shots outside shattered the silence.

But they hadn't come from the back of the house where Mike had gone. They'd come from the side.

I'll go out there, draw their attention by not using a silencer on my gun and lead them away, Zee had said to him.

No! *What have you done?*

RYKER AND HIS MEN were creeping up onto the porch, preparing to breach the house from different ingress points when four shots rang out.

Raising his fist in the air, he silently told his guys to hold. He backed down the steps and hurried in the direction from where the shots had come.

Zee jumped from the porch and ran, headed for the woods.

"You three with me," Ryker said to some of his men and then looked at the other two. "The rest of you, find my daughter. Kill anyone who gets in your way."

He turned and took off at a mad dash toward the woods. She might have a head start, but he was so much faster. And she had no one to help her.

This was a chase he would savor.

Kicking into a sprint, he ran flat out, his long legs eating up the distance between them. Nothing on earth was going to stop him from catching her. Nothing and no one.

"Zenobia!"

JOHN MADE IT to the second-floor landing as Delta burst in through the front door.

Right on time, the generator switched on, flooding the house in bright light. The men reeled back, trying to adjust their NVGs.

John raised Big Betty and pumped slugs into each of them, taking the two of them down. He waited for more men storm in.

But none came.

Zee.

He raced up the stairs and pain flared from his thigh to his shin. His leg was killing him. He had to hop and use the railing for leverage up the steps, but he blocked out the discomfort and moved as fast as his body would carry him.

In the bedroom, the window was open. A bone-chilling breeze swept through the room. Zee was gone.

He rushed to the window, propped Big Betty up on the edge of the headboard and looked through the scope.

It took him a moment to focus and scan the property.

There!

Zee dashed into the woods. Trench Coat—*Ryker*—disappeared into the tree line seconds after her. Too fast for John to take a shot.

His molten rage bled into an icy calm. Sighting through the scope, John took a deep breath, finger on the trigger, exhaled. Waited.

A Delta operative sprinting toward the woods came into his crosshairs. He pulled the trigger. A shot rang out and the man dropped.

Another was still running in the same direction.

John aimed and squeezed. That one crumpled to the ground, too.

The third man who had been in pursuit changed his course wildly, heading back to the house, but he was out in the open. Nowhere to hide. Nowhere to run.

One shot and John took him out. He scanned the area.

Once he was sure there was no one else, he bolted for the staircase and rushed down the steps. On the main floor, he hopped over the dead bodies and raced outside. The children would be safe. So would Mike and Enola.

But Zee was out in the woods, injured and alone, with Ryker.

Chapter Twenty

Ignoring the cramping in her side, Zee extended her legs and pumped her arms, running with everything that she had.

Footfalls pounded after her. Getting louder. Gaining. Drawing closer.

She didn't dare look back. It'd only slow her down and she knew what she would see.

Ryker's face. Enraged. Bloodthirsty.

Adrenaline surged through her bloodstream, spurring her on. She darted around a tree, zigzagging to avoid capture, her feet striking the ground faster and faster.

He swore at her. Cursed her. Raved like a lunatic. She could hear his breathing now he was so close. Strong. Steady.

Relentless.

Panic swept through her as her heart raced. Her lungs burned. Her breath punched white into the air. Her legs screamed. Her arm ached with a gut-wrenching agony that would feel like nothing in comparison to what Ryker would do to her if he got his hands on her.

She had to get away. Had to keep going. Had to run faster. But he was closing in on her too quickly. He wouldn't stop until she was dead. Or she killed him first.

The toe of her boot caught, and she lurched forward, her arms flailing, trying to regain her balance.

"Careful," a deep voice said from behind her, "don't fall and break your neck." Powerful arms hooked around her waist, snatching her from the ground.

Her heart seized in her throat.

"I want the pleasure of doing it." His hot breath was in her ear.

Oh, God! No! He had her.

Screaming, she kicked and swung her fists, but only hit air. He knocked her gun from her hand. Not that it mattered. She was out of bullets.

His grip was tight, painful, punishing. Ryker spun them both and threw her to the ground onto her back. He pounced on top of her.

The wind was knocked from her lungs. But that didn't stop her. On pure instinct, her training kicking in, she punched straight out.

Ryker pulled back out of reach. Then he grabbed her by her hair, yanking her head up from the ground and slammed it down, again and again, banging her skull into the hard frozen earth.

Dazed, hurting, she tried to focus on something. Anything. But her vision swam, and her mind was thick from the blows to her head.

Ryker was sputtering vile things, straddling her. His hips had her legs pinned.

She howled in frustration. In a fight, fist to fist, she didn't stand a snowball's chance in hell. A woman's ultimate power came from her lower body, where she was strongest, and a well-aimed kick was her greatest weapon.

And Ryker knew it.

Grabbing the hilt of her baton, she yanked it from the holster on her hip and flicked it out to its full length. As she swung up with her right hand, Ryker snatched her wrist. With his other hand, he seized her throat, pinching her windpipe closed.

She gasped. Involuntarily without thinking, she clawed at his arm bearing down on her throat. But it was no use. He was too strong, and she was in the weakest position possible.

He twisted her wrist a half turn counterclockwise. The pressure and the pain made her open her fingers and drop the baton before he broke the bone.

She would have shrieked in agony if she had been capable of making any sound.

"I gave you everything and you didn't appreciate any of it!" Exertion and rage turned Ryker's face red. "I rescued you from that hacktivist group in Germany. Kept you out of prison. Gave you a career at the CIA. Spared you my darker proclivities in bed because I knew they would scare you. Made you a mother. Gave you a baby. And you repaid me by taking everything from me!" He tightened his hold around her throat. "Instead of despising me, you should have worshipped me!"

Gagging, Zee wheezed for air. Darkness tugged

at her consciousness, creeping around the edges of her vision. She couldn't give in to it. She had to fight.

She needed to breathe. *Oh, please, not like this. Not by his hand.* Ryker was killing her.

What would happen to Olivia? Her baby girl. Her precious child. The one good, true thing that came from this evil monster.

Protect her, John.

"Not once did you ever thank me!" Ryker loomed over her, bearing down. "Or show me the gratitude that I deserve. But you will now." He eased up on her throat, slowly, letting go.

She sucked in air and coughed. Her heart throbbed in her chest. The blackness receded.

Then he put a gun to her head.

Click!

The distinctive sound of the hammer being cocked echoed through her brain.

"Keep fighting me and I'll pull the trigger right now," he promised.

Fear thickened her blood. Wrestling against every instinct to protect herself, she stilled.

"Apologize for not loving me. Tell me you're sorry for throwing away our family. Then I want you to beg." He dragged the nose of the weapon from her head, along her throat, down farther. "Beg me for your life." He pushed the muzzle into her gunshot wound.

Squeezing her eyes shut as tears leaked out, she screamed in anguish.

"Start by saying you're sorry. Do it if you want me to treat our daughter well."

She looked at him and bile flooded her throat. Then her gaze drifted to the gun pressed to her injured arm.

But she saw something else, too.

A Ka-Bar knife holstered on his hip.

"I'm sorry," she cried, relaxing her body, spoon-feeding his confidence that he'd already won, and he watched her intently, pleasure gleaming in his sick eyes, his smiling face aglow with triumph that twisted her stomach into a knot. "Sorry for everything I did wrong. But most of all... I'm so, so sorry that I didn't kill you in your sleep."

She drew the knife from the holster and plunged the blade into him and twisted. He dropped the gun, but she'd missed her target, hitting his shoulder.

Quickly, she yanked the serrated blade out and aimed for his black heart.

But Ryker slapped her backhanded, and the Ka-Bar flew from her grip.

Roaring in pain, he reared back and clenched his hand to strike her.

But she launched a fist first to his throat. She bucked her hips, thrusting him off her as he choked and with both feet kicked him farther away. Putting distance between them, she crawled on her butt backward across the ground. She felt around for his gun or her baton.

She had to kill him if it was the last thing she ever did. Ryker had to die. Tonight.

"I'm going to tear you into pieces!" Ryker said, recovering.

Curling her fingers around the hilt of her baton, she braced herself. *Go for his knees, groin, head.*

Ryker charged at her. Growling. Snarling. Teeth bared. Ready to hurt her. To kill her.

Movement rushed in from the side. *John.* He tackled Ryker to the ground.

Zee scurried to a tree and pulled herself up along the trunk.

The two men wrestled, rolling around, throwing punches and kicking each other. She scrambled for Ryker's gun. There was no way that monster was leaving this forest alive.

In a lightning-fast move, John seized Ryker from behind, locking him in a position with the psycho's back to his chest. He snaked an arm around Ryker's throat and wrapped his legs around the man's hips. The struggle only lasted a second longer before John snapped Ryker's neck.

A rush of relief cascaded through her, a dam of terror breaking inside her.

She sobbed, collapsing to her knees. At last, she was free of Ryker Rudin.

John tossed the limp body to the side. Standing, he stumbled to her, dropped to her side and wrapped her in his arms. "The children are safe. The rest of Delta are dead. Are you okay?"

No, no, she wasn't. But… "I will be." She hugged him back, vowing never to let him go.

He lifted her to her feet, throwing his arm around her. Hugging her tight, he kissed her cheeks and her head. He inspected her face and grimaced and kissed her again.

They started making their way back to the house, clinging to each other and slogging along.

"I have to contact Hunter," she said, "and we have to leave before another team shows up. Mike will need to call the cops as soon as we're gone."

"Yeah, okay." He tightened his arm around her. They reached the house and he said, "You do realize you reneged on our deal."

"What? How so?"

"I told you to wait for me," he said, "and you agreed."

"I never agreed. You believed what you wanted."

"You neglected to tell me you weren't waiting and omitted that you'd planned to go out the window. But I'll cut you some slack this one time, and we'll consider it a gray area."

"You know what's not gray?"

"What?"

"How much I love you."

Chapter Twenty-One

Six weeks later...

John walked through the main house on the island off the coast of Venezuela. Hunter Wright's house. It was less than a mile down the beach from the hut that he lived in with Zee and Olivia, and about half a mile away from Gage Graham and Hope Fischer's place.

The island was a slice of paradise. Balmy San Diego weather. In the daytime, seventy-five degrees Fahrenheit and at night the lows dipped into the sixties. Mild breezes. Fresh air, plenty of fish, seafood and produce. A powdery-soft sand beach that he took long walks on every day, most of the time with Zee. His afternoons he spent swimming and helping homeschool Olivia.

He even got on well with the guys from her team and Hope was a nice lady. Best of all, he got to wake up every morning with Zee in his arms, curled up next to him.

Paradise.

Three or four times a week, like this evening,

they all gathered for a family-style dinner at Hunter's house.

John entered the dining room, where Olivia was setting the table. "Need any help?"

"No, I've got it," she said, giving him a bright smile.

He pitched in anyway, folding napkins and arranging them beside the plates. "How did your Mandarin lesson go with Hunter?"

She rattled off something in Chinese and then in English said, "He says I'm a natural."

"Of course you are." The eleven-year-old already spoke Spanish, Zee was teaching her German, and now Mandarin. Her incredible brain was like a giant sponge, soaking in everything and retaining it. Boggled his mind, but he couldn't be any prouder of her. "Since the table is finished, why don't we sit outside and wait for your mom to get back."

Hunter was usually the only one who made trips to the mainland to stock up on supplies, to limit the exposure of the rest of their merry little band, but Zee had insisted on being the one to go today.

"Sure." Olivia led the way with a bounce in her step that brought a smile to his face.

He liked seeing his ladies happy. It made him happy.

"Can we play Dungeons & Dragons tonight?" Olivia asked.

The game was addictive. "I'm up for it. We can see if your mom is interested, but I bet Gage will be in."

They stepped outside onto the wraparound veranda and took a seat side by side on the porch swing.

"What does the air smell like here?" he asked her.

"The ocean and plumeria. I love that flower. I asked Mom if she'd buy me some perfume with that scent while she was on the mainland."

"What did she say?"

Olivia shrugged and pouted. "She'll think about it."

"Well, that's not a no."

"It's not a yes either."

John chuckled. "Hey, I wanted to talk to you about something before your mom gets back."

Olivia tilted her head to the side and looked at him. "About what?"

"I wanted to get your permission."

Perking up with a straight back, she leaned in. "I'm usually the one who has to ask permission."

"Not this time." He took a deep breath. "I want to propose to your mom, but since this concerns the three of us, I thought I should—"

"Yes!" she said with a squeal of delight and threw her arms around his neck, yanked him down in a stranglehold of a hug. "Yes, you have my permission." She let him go and pulled back. "So, would that make you my dad?"

"I'd be honored if you thought of me as such." He already considered her his daughter. "Once I marry your mom, provided she says yes," he said, also knowing they had to clear Zee's name, "I'd like to officially adopt you." Every decision he made centered around Zee and Olivia. His family. He loved them both and would die to protect them.

"I never knew my dad. Mom said he was a bad person who did bad things and that he'd never be in my life. It'll be nice to finally have one." Olivia looked at him and beamed. "Did you already get her a ring?"

"Sure did." He reached into his pocket and took out the ring box. "Do you want to see it?"

"Do birds fly?"

He pulled the ring box back. "Well, now I'm not so sure if I should show it to you since not all birds do fly. Penguins, weka—"

"Ostriches, kiwi, cassowary. Come on, John, it was a figure of speech. Don't hold it against me. I want to see it." She rubbed her palms together, her bright brown eyes gleaming.

"Okay," he said, handing her the black box, "but only because you redeemed yourself."

She flipped up the lid and gasped. "Wow!"

It was a round, brilliant cut solitary diamond. One point seven carats that glinted fire. Perfect for Zee. Hunter had hawked John's watch for him so he could pay for it under the ruse that the watch needed to be repaired.

On the run he didn't have access to his bank account, investments or disability payments, and he didn't want to wait until the situation with Team Topaz was resolved.

He had no idea how long it could take, and he wanted to make Zee his wife and claim Olivia as his daughter, officially, as soon as possible.

Life was too short to delay something this special.

"Do you think she'll say yes?" he asked.

"Oh, I know she will." Olivia closed the lid and handed him the box. "She loves you. And you really love her, too, don't you?"

"I love your mom with all my heart, from the bottom of my soul straight to my gut. My only reason for breathing is to make her happy. I love you, too, and I'd do anything for you both."

"When are you going to ask her?"

"I was thinking tonight. Should I do it at dinner in front of everyone or in private on the beach? What do you think she'd prefer?"

John had already given this considerable thought. Zee loved her teammates. They were family, people who cared for her and would do anything to keep her safe and vice versa. But she valued her privacy, as well. A wedding he could envision in front of everyone, but he suspected Zee would prefer an intimate moment. Just the two of them.

Nothing was set in stone and he wanted Olivia to have a chance to share her opinion. It was important to him to make sure she was a part of the process every step of the way and never felt excluded.

"On the beach at sunset," Olivia said. "Mom will be shocked, and she'll probably cry and wouldn't want anyone else to see. And if she says no that'll spare you any embarrassment."

John's smile fell. Unease churned in his gut. That last part about her rejecting him hadn't crossed his mind. "Do you think she might say no?"

Olivia elbowed his side and giggled. "I'm just messing with you."

He chuckled.

The roar of an outboard motor buzzed in the air drawing both their gazes to the water.

"Mom's back!" Olivia jumped up and ran to the rail of the veranda and waved.

A speedboat with Zee behind the wheel zipped along the water's surface heading in their direction.

John stood, going to stand beside her. "Remember, not a word."

"I'm good at keeping secrets."

Both of his ladies were and didn't he know it.

They strolled down the beach to meet her on the dock and unload any supplies. The sun was low on the horizon, painting the sky red, gold and purple.

Zee's hair was loose and wild, blowing in the wind, her sundress fluttering along with the breeze. She slowed as she got closer and brought the boat alongside the dock. The breeze carried the vessel right in to where it needed to be. She cut the engine on the speedboat as John grabbed a line. He tossed it to her, and she tied up.

Offering his hand, he helped her climb out and up onto the dock. He noticed there were no crates or bags in the boat. Pulling her into his body, he kissed her.

"Did you get it for me, Mom?" Olivia bounced up and down on the balls of her feet with her fingers crossed. "Please tell me you got me perfume."

"Repeat it in Spanish," Zee said.

Olivia sighed and then did as she was instructed.

Zee rewarded her with a small roll-on bottle of perfume.

"Gracias." She hugged her mother. "Enjoy the sunset." With a wave, she ran off with the bottle back to the house.

John slipped his arm around Zee's shoulder, tucking her against his side. They left the dock and hit the beach. "Did you have a good trip?" He ran his fingers across her healed gunshot wound, and renewed gratitude that she was alive and well filled him.

"I did."

It was hard to miss the absence of supplies. "Are you going to tell me what you went to the mainland for?"

She opened her bohemian cloth handbag, and John peered inside as she pulled out a medicine bottle.

He spotted a rectangular box with distinctive blue-and-white packaging, Clearblue, in a plastic bag.

She handed him the pills. "The refill will last you a month."

Dropping his arm, he stopped and stared at her. "Sweetheart, could you be pregnant?"

Was it possible?

Well, of course it was. It only took one time and they had enjoyed each other every single night and there had been a few afternoons as well when Olivia was at the main house.

"Oh, gosh no." Zee recoiled. "I'm not. That's not for me, but that is the real reason I went to the mainland. Hope didn't want any of the guys to know, until she knew for certain, so play dumb."

"Okay," he said, sounding relieved, but what he felt was closer to an ache of disappointment.

"The test will confirm what I already know. Hope is pregnant. That's why I also got her these." She showed him a bottle of prenatal vitamins.

"How do you know for sure that she's pregnant?"

"She's two weeks late, suddenly nauseous all the time and her breasts have gotten a little bigger."

Thankfully he hadn't noticed any of that. He wondered if Gage had? Would John if their situations were reversed?

"Are you sure you couldn't be?" John asked.

"Relax, big guy." She put a palm on his chest and rubbed. "I'm positive. After what happened with Ryker," she said, her gaze falling, "I got an IUD. Mine won't need to be replaced until next year. You don't need to worry about me trapping you." She smirked.

"Do you want more kids?" They'd talked about a future together once their names were cleared, discussed money, politics, religion. Had asked each other a thousand questions.

Marriage was about a million different compromises. Things that they'd never think to ask would come up. Life was capable of throwing some wicked sucker punches.

But for some reason this one question hadn't been mentioned.

He didn't even realize he wanted to have a baby with her someday until this moment. What if she didn't want to go through the dirty diapers and lack of sleep all over again?

She wrapped her arms around his waist and pulled them pelvis to pelvis. "I'm open to the possibility. With the right guy. At the right time." She rose on her toes and brushed her nose across his before kissing him. "Do you?" she asked, lowering back to the sand.

"I want to be trapped with you and have babies and raise Olivia and grow old with you." All of that came out completely wrong.

"John."

He'd started and might as well finish, so he whipped out the ring box.

Zee staggered back, her hand flying to her chest.

Opening the lid, he lowered to his good knee. "I've been with a lot of women," he said, and she frowned at him. Taking a deep breath, he mentally kicked himself and tried again. "What I mean is, you're the only woman that I've ever loved. Just looking at you makes me smile and fills me with a joy I've never known before. You make life worth living. You make me want to be a better man for you and for Olivia. Marry me."

Her jaw dropped as she stared at him. "Are you sure? I'm a package deal with a lot of baggage. I'm a fugitive."

He stood in front of her. "I've never been more certain of anything in my life. I love you and Olivia. I want both of you to be my family. No, you already are my family. I want to make it official, permanent, for the two of you to take my name. And I promise to cherish what we've found together, what we're creating, every day of my life. Marry me, Zenobia."

Tears welled up in her eyes. "Yes, I'll marry you."

She leaned in, twining her arms around his neck, tangling her fingers in his hair, and kissed him.

As he soaked in the warmth of her body, the beat of her heart against his chest, the kiss was familiar and new all at once. Like the first time. Like coming home.

This was right. In Alaska, he'd felt a connection to her that he couldn't explain. One that made no sense. But now he understood, she was the other part of him. A kindred spirit. The two of them, make that the three of them, together made all the sense in the world.

"I finally understand why my mom never complained about living in Breezy Point. She used to tell me that it didn't matter if she was in Antarctica or Bed-Stuyvesant. That as long as she was with my dad then that was where she belonged. That's what you are for me, John. You're my shelter and when I'm with you I feel at home. I want to be yours forever."

Happy tears rolled down her cheeks as he slid the ring on her finger. Cupping her face in his hands, he kissed her again and tasted the salt of her tears.

Applause and cheers had them both turning toward the house. Olivia, Hunter, Gage and Hope were all out on the veranda watching them.

With his arm around her shoulder and hers curled around his waist, they strolled up to the house.

"Is your watch really getting repaired or did you have Hunter pawn it to buy my engagement ring?"

He smiled at her. "It's no big deal."

"But it is. I know what it meant to you."

"You mean more. Besides, I know who I am, and

I'll never forget it again. I've got T.O.T.S. branded on my heart."

They walked up the steps of the veranda.

"We're getting married!" Olivia said, and everyone laughed.

Congratulations, pats on the back, handshakes, hugs and compliments on the ring were given. Zee and Hope deftly maneuvered down the porch for a moment. Using their bodies to shield their exchange, Zee passed Hope the Clearblue in the plastic bag and the other woman slipped the package into her purse.

The other men seemed none the wiser with their backs turned, but once the ladies rejoined the group, Hunter's gaze bounced between them like he was aware something was up.

Everyone moseyed into the house for dinner and grabbed a seat around the table. There was a spread of grilled fish, octopus, arepas—griddle-fried corn cakes, rice, black beans and loads of vegetables.

Hunter grabbed a bottle of champagne and popped the cork, which made Hope visibly nervous, and poured bubbly in flutes.

Hope pushed her glass away. "None for me, thank you."

"Stomach flu still bothering you?" Hunter asked.

"Yeah." She nodded.

Gage sucked back a glass of champagne and took hers. "If it doesn't clear up in the next day or two, it might be a parasite."

"That's one possibility," Hunter said. "Though I doubt that's what it is."

"Do you think it's something more serious?" Gage asked.

The corner of Hunter's mouth hitched in a half grin. "I think it's something that won't *clear up* anytime soon."

Apparently, Gage and John had been the only clueless ones. John felt bad for Gage. He was the only grown-up at the table who didn't know.

The phone in Hunter's office rang, and a hush fell over the table. It was the first time he'd heard any phone ring since they had arrived on the island.

Hunter got up, putting his napkin down, and hurried to the office. He answered the phone. "Parachute."

"It's Dean," Zee said.

"Does that mean he's in some kind of trouble the way you were?" John asked.

Under the table, she took his hand. "Unfortunately, it does."

Hunter rattled off coordinates and instructions, wished him good luck and hung up. A minute later, he returned to the table and sat. "Dean may be joining us soon, depending on how things shake out for him."

Around the table there were grim faces and crestfallen looks.

"Isn't this a good thing?" John asked. "Your team is stronger together than apart."

"Every teammate who arrives exponentially increases the odds of us being discovered," Hunter said. "If Dean makes it, and I hope that he does, because he's in serious trouble, then I think it might be time to stop hiding and take this fight to Langley's door before they bring it here."

"Yes." John pounded a fist on table, drawing everyone's attention. "We go to the mattresses."

Hunter nodded. "We'll go to war and we won't stop until we clear our names."

Confirmation of everything David Bertrand had shared with them before he died was on Zee's hard drive. But due to the money in the offshore accounts, it wasn't enough evidence to exonerate them. They had to find out who wanted Ashref Saleh dead and why. Then they could track down the proof they needed.

David's death wasn't in vain. Thanks to him, Team Topaz knew what they were looking for and where to start.

Zee squeezed John's hand tighter and glanced across the table at Olivia.

John would figure out a way to keep Olivia out of the crosshairs and make sure she was safe. He leaned into Zee and whispered, "As long as we're together…" Nothing else mattered.

He knew how to endure, and she knew how to fight. Together they were whole. Stronger, better than apart.

She looked at him with pure love in her eyes. "We can get through anything."

* * * * *

Look for the next book in Juno Rushdan's
Fugitive Heroes: Topaz Unit series,
Disavowed in Wyoming

And don't miss the previous book in the series:
Rogue Christmas Operation
Available from Harlequin Intrigue!

WE HOPE YOU ENJOYED
THIS BOOK FROM

HARLEQUIN
INTRIGUE

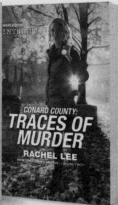

Seek thrills. Solve crimes. Justice served.

Dive into action-packed stories that will keep you
on the edge of your seat. Solve the crime
and deliver justice at all costs.

6 NEW BOOKS AVAILABLE EVERY MONTH!

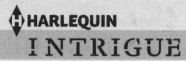

#2043 PURSUED BY THE SHERIFF
Mercy Ridge Lawmen • by Delores Fossen

The bullet that rips through Sheriff Jace Castillo's body stalls his investigation. But being nursed back to health by the shooter's sister is his biggest complication yet. Linnea Martell has always been—and still is—off-limits. And the danger only intensifies when Linnea gets caught in the line of fire...

#2044 DISAPPEARANCE AT DAKOTA RIDGE
Eagle Mountain: Search for Suspects • by Cindi Myers

When Lauren Baker's sister-in-law and niece go missing, she immediately has a suspect in mind and heads to Eagle Mountain, where she turns to Deputy Shane Ellis for help. And when another woman seen with her family is found dead, their desperate pursuit for answers becomes even more urgent.

#2045 COWBOY IN THE CROSSHAIRS
A North Star Novel Series • by Nicole Helm

After attempting to expose corruption throughout the military, former navy SEAL Nate Averly becomes an assassin's next target. When he flees to his brother's Montana ranch, North Star agent Elsie Rogers must protect him and uncover the threat before more lives are lost. But they're up against a cunning adversary who's deadlier than they ever imagined...

#2046 DISAVOWED IN WYOMING
Fugitive Heroes: Topaz Unit • by Juno Rushdan

Fleeing from a CIA kill squad, former operative Dean Delgado finds himself back in Wyoming and befriending veterinarian Kate Sawyer—the woman he was once forced to leave behind. But when an emergency call brings Kate under fire, protecting her is the only mission that matters to Dean—even if it puts his own life at risk.

#2047 LITTLE GIRL GONE
A Procedural Crime Story • by Amanda Stevens

Special agent Thea Lamb returns to her hometown to search for a child whose disappearance echoes a twenty-eight-year-old cold case—her twin sister's abduction. Working with her former partner, Jake Stillwell, Thea must overcome the pain that has tormented her for years. For both Thea and Jake, the job always came first...until now.

#2048 CHASING THE VIOLET KILLER
by R. Barri Flowers

After witnessing a serial killer murder her relative live on video chat, Secret Service agent Naomi Lincoln is determined to solve the case. But investigating forces her to work with detective Dylan Hester—the boyfriend she left brokenhearted years ago. Capturing the Violet Killer will be the greatest challenge of their lives—especially once he sets his sights on Naomi.

"If need be, I could run my way out of these woods. You can't
run," Linnea added.

"No, but I can return fire if we get into trouble," Jace argued.
"And I stand a better chance of hitting a target than you do."

It was a good argument. Well, it would have been if he
hadn't had the gunshot wound. It wasn't on his shooting arm,
thank goodness, but he was weak, and any movement could
cause that wound to open up.

"You could bleed out before I get you out of these woods,"
Linnea reminded him. "Besides, I'm not sure you can shoot,
much less shoot straight. You can't even stand up without help."

As if to prove her wrong, he picked up his gun from the
nightstand and straightened his posture, pulling back his
shoulders.

And what little color he had drained from his face.

Cursing him and their situation, she dragged a chair closer
to the window and had him sit down.

"The main road isn't that far, only about a mile," she
continued. Linnea tried to tamp down her argumentative tone.
"I can get there on the ATV and call for help. Your deputies and

the EMTs can figure out the best way to get you to a hospital."

That was the part of her plan that worked. What she didn't feel comfortable about was leaving Jace alone while she got to the main road. Definitely not ideal, but they didn't have any other workable solutions.

Of course, this option wouldn't work until the lightning stopped. She could get through the wind and rain, but if she got struck by lightning or a tree falling from a strike, it could be fatal. First to her, and then to Jace, since he'd be stuck here in the cabin.

He looked up at her, his color a little better now, and his eyes were hard and intense. "I can't let you take a risk like that. Gideon could ambush you."

"That's true," she admitted. "But the alternative is for us to wait here. Maybe for days until you're strong enough to ride out with me. That might not be wise since I suspect you need antibiotics for your wound before an infection starts brewing."

His jaw tightened, and even though he'd had plenty trouble standing, Jace got up. This time he didn't stagger, but she did notice the white-knuckle grip he had on his gun. "We'll see how I feel once the storm has passed."

In other words, he would insist on going with her. Linnea sighed. Obviously, Jace had a mile-wide stubborn streak and was planning on dismissing her *one workable option*.

"If you're hungry, there's some canned soup in the cabinet," she said, shifting the subject.

Jace didn't respond to that. However, he did step in front of her as if to shield her. And he lifted his gun.

"Get down," Jace ordered. "Someone's out there."

Don't miss
Pursued by the Sheriff
*by Delores Fossen, available January 2022 wherever
Harlequin Intrigue books and ebooks are sold.*

Harlequin.com

HIEXP1221

Get 4 FREE REWARDS!

We'll send you 2 FREE Books plus <u>2 FREE</u> Mystery Gifts.

Harlequin Intrigue books are action-packed stories that will keep you on the edge of your seat. Solve the crime and deliver justice at all costs.

FREE Value Over **$20**

"All of that's true and I hate this has happened to you,"
Maxwell said. "But you've forgotten one important fact.
You weren't harmed. At least not physically. Everything
in that house can be replaced."

"That might be true, but—"

"But you—" he kissed the side of her forehead
"—sweetheart, you're irreplaceable, and I'm glad you
weren't hurt. Now, *that*? That would've made the evening
a helluva lot worse. Because if that had happened, I
would be out for blood. We wouldn't be sitting here
together because I'd be out hunting that bastard. Instead,
we have others looking into the situation while you and I
are getting ready to try to salvage our date. So how about
we start by enjoying an excellent meal?"

After a long beat of silence, Amina sighed dramatically and leaned back to look up at him. A slow smile tugged the corners of her lips. "Well, when you put it that way, I guess I should pick a restaurant, huh?"

He grinned and handed her the menus. "Yes, and I'll take the bags upstairs, then change clothes. When I come back down, we can order." He stood and headed for the stairs again but stopped when she called him. "Yeah?"

"Thanks for coming to the house. It meant a lot to have you there with me even though I know it was the last place you wanted to be."

He studied her for a moment. "That might've been the case at first, but I want to be wherever you are, Amina. And I'll always be here, there or wherever for you. Remember that."

Don't miss
His to Defend *by Sharon C. Cooper,*
available January 2022 wherever
Harlequin Romantic Suspense
books and ebooks are sold.

Harlequin.com